ONCE

upon a Twice

To Muditha & Leo
Warm Wishes
Santhoshya Seneviratne
Sep 29, 2019

SANTHOSHYA JAYAMALI SENEVIRATNE

ONCE UPON A TWICE

Copyright © 2018 by Santhoshya Seneviratne

Tellwell Talent

www.tellwell.ca

ISBN

978-0-2288-0952-4 (Hardcover)

978-0-2288-0055-2 (Paperback)

978-0-2288-0955-5 (eBook)

To all those who find
themselves centuries in the past.

If you ask me what I came to do in this world, I, an artist, will answer you: I am here to live out loud.
ÉMILE ZOLA, attributed, *And I Quote*

If you shut up truth and bury it under the ground, it will but grow, and gather to itself such explosive power that the day it bursts through it will blow up everything in its way.
ÉMILE ZOLA, attributed, *Dreyfus: His Life and Letters*

The past was but the cemetery of our illusions: one simply stubbed one's toes on the gravestones.
ÉMILE ZOLA, *The Masterpiece*

There are two men inside the artist, the poet and the craftsman. One is born a poet. One becomes a craftsman.
ÉMILE ZOLA, letter to Paul Cézanne

Everything is only a dream.
ÉMILE ZOLA, *Le Rêve*

My fiery protest is simply the cry of my very soul.
ÉMILE ZOLA, *"J'accuse…!"*

Preface

Émile Zola was a controversial French novelist and also a major figure in political liberty. He was the proponent of Naturalism, famous for his great works like *Germinal* (1885), *La Bête Humaine* (1890), *L'Oeuvre* (1886), *L'Assommoir* (1877), *Thérèse Raquin* (1867) and *Au Bonheur des Dames* (1883).

In 1898, in the newspaper *L'Aurore*, he published *J'Accuse…!*, an open letter to the president of France, Félix Faure, with the sole intention of proving the innocence of Alfred Dreyfus, an artillery officer who was wrongfully accused of treason, tried twice and consecutively jailed both times. Alfred Dreyfus, cleared of all his accusations, was released after Zola's death, caused by carbon monoxide poisoning in 1902.

Once Upon A Twice is a story that deals with high levels of parallelism between history and the present. The story deals with Zola's attraction towards Jeanne Rozerot, a seamstress who worked in his house, in parallel with the close association between a modern-day professor of performing arts—who releases a screenplay derived from Zola's famous short story, *Pour Une Nuit D'Amour*—and a young girl, a writer, who visits him to work on it.

The professor unknowingly finds himself in Zola, and he directs his writer to investigate the history and uncover facts about the great novelist, Émile Zola. She follows instructions and ends up finding herself there, as well as the professor. She can't help but see the same veins, temperaments, and loneliness that accompanied Zola, in the professor, who gives weight to Zola's character creation, Julien, in *Pour Une Nuit D'Amour*. And most amazingly, a series of events take place between the professor and his writer, emphasizing the same or similar events that took place between Zola and Jeanne Rozerot more than a century ago, together with the characters in *Pour Une Nuit D'Amour*.

The young writer understands the professor in depth. With her sympathetic, empathetic heart, she understands his need to be understood, while the professor identifies himself in Zola. Just by studying him, he sees the same need to overcome his loneliness. They spontaneously and most effortlessly find themselves in the two historical characters, ending up in a similar predicament.

I've excluded any particular setting or names of characters in the modern-day story to highlight its universality. It's a story that can happen to anyone, anywhere in the world.

Santhoshya Jayamali Seneviratne

19th–20th Century

She stood on the other side of the road trying to decide if it was the right time to advance, not knowing that she was taking time to decide something else. She did have a slight inkling but thought it was just a passing sentiment, so she gave it no more thought.

There were only a few vehicles on the road, but she didn't make a move. Something kept her standing still. Was she lethargic? Not really, she was just withdrawn. Her eyes were directed at a house that stood on the other side of the road. It was massive. There seemed to be two tall towers on either side, connected by a rectangular slab, but it was just one building. She thought she was going to be lost there. It was much larger than her home.

She looked down, unable to bear the glare of it, wondering why she hesitated and tried to take the whole house in at once. The tower on the left, with its many windows and triangular roof, was right to stand by itself. The tower on the right looked like an upright rectangle without a shelter. The rectangular slab in the middle was definitely just a common area of the house that could stand alone. The house was remarkable, however, with windows in abundance and with the appearance of three houses attached together.

She wondered where the main entrance was and guessed that it was on the left. She stood there, not moving her eyes away, and with a quick struggle made her decision. The road was crossed quickly, and she walked her way over, finding herself there in no time.

She tiptoed along the narrow path, still looking at the building; it was a struggle now, so she aimed her eyes at what they saw directly in front of her and ended up looking at the windows. Soon, she was at the entrance: a massive door with carvings and a huge metal door knocker right above the lock.

She still hesitated before she made any sound, wondering if she was making the right decision by taking up the new occupation, then felt the rusted knocker in her hand. A smile appeared on her face at the touch of it, and she quickly made her move, making the loudest knock. The door opened much sooner than she expected and a middle-aged woman who looked like a servant stood there.

"Jeanne Rozerot?"

"Yes," she replied.

"Madame has been waiting for you. Come on in!"

She walked inside, and the woman closed the door.

"I'm Anette, working in the kitchen," the servant said. "You can hang your coat there and let's go meet her first."

Jeanne hung her coat on the hook and started following Anette. A few questions were asked by the servant on their brief walk to the living room, and she answered modestly.

"Have you ever worked in a house before?"

"No. This is my first time in a house."

"Where did you work earlier?"

"Just with dressmakers in town."

"So, you like to work in a house?"

"Yes, it's more comfortable."

"Lots of sewing got collected 'cause we haven't had a seamstress for a long time."

Jeanne was silent. She wondered why a seamstress had to be employed in a house where there didn't seem to be a lot of people living. But she never questioned it. She would happily take on the job, although that subtle reluctance existed within her, for a reason that hadn't yet crossed her mind.

They walked along the hallway and entered an open area that took them to the large living room. It was bright with large windows, and her first guess was that it was placed in the middle of the horizontal rectangle.

"Madame, she's here."

Anette spoke loudly, but Jeanne couldn't see anyone there until a lady who was sitting in an armchair turned her head to see the new seamstress. She was seated at the fireplace facing the opposite direction, so she could hardly be seen.

With no solid reason, Jeanne was alarmed when she saw her. It was a sudden fright, brought about by feelings of premonition. Their eyes met. Well, it was an excellent meeting. One wasn't above, below or similar to the other. Alexandrine, the lady of the house, was definitely well past her middle age while the little seamstress was just reaching the prime of her youth.

Jeanne had her eyes on Alexandrine for some time before a conversation began. Alexandrine was a stout lady with hair tied in a topknot. She looked tired. The hot beverage she was sipping was soothing her. The long light-coloured dress she wore matched her present temperament. Jeanne thought she was unhappy, for some reason. She was a woman whose weariness was at its highest. Also, she looked extremely exhausted. Jeanne kept her eyes focused on the collar of her dress. It had a beautiful cross-stitch pattern on it, and she noticed the same stitching on the long sleeves of the dress. Despite her fatigue, there was a smile on her face. It was an eternal smile, although there were specific moments mingled with it.

Alexandrine had all her senses at work, just like Jeanne did. The young seamstress was a little lovely. She was bubbling in her youth, looking like she was just ready for some responsible work. However, she wondered if a girl as young as Jeanne could manage all the sewing of the house by herself. She had no doubt about it whatsoever.

It was a long moment of silence, and Jeanne broke it at last.

"Bonjour madame."

"Bonjour and come sit down here! Some things to make clear before you start."

Jeanne made the best of the little invitation and made herself sit down at a distance. She felt too small to sit any closer to Alexandrine, and also, she didn't want her inner reluctance disclosed.

Alexandrine asked her very first question: "Have you ever worked for a household before?"

"No, this is my first time in a house," Jeanne replied.

Anette smiled, almost reading the young girl's mind. Jeanne didn't stop at that. She continued her explanation.

"I worked for the dressmakers in town and completed many orders for them."

"Where did you go to school?"

"Rouvres-sous-Meilly Public School, madame, and I completed my last grade just two years ago."

"I see."

Alexandrine didn't look like she had any more questions. Even her straightforward questions made it sound like she didn't even want to know anything about her.

"Anette." She called the servant to her.

"Oui?"

"You can first get this girl something to drink before you show her the sewing room."

"Oui, madame."

Anette made a slight gesture, and Jeanne stood up to follow her again. They walked all the way to the kitchen where Jeanne was shown a little table. Anette asked her to sit down. It was a table with a few chairs that looked like it was kept there for the workers of the house. Soon, she was served with a warm drink. The weather was cold, so she began to sip it.

"Take your time, and I'll be back soon."

Anette left, and Jeanne sipped the drink, examining the room. Everything around her was beautiful, and she felt very comfortable. When she was done with the drink, Anette came back. The two workers started towards the sewing room, and that was what Jeanne had really wanted. They walked further to the interior of the house where she was shown a large room in a cozy little corner.

"This is your sewing room. You can take time and familiarize yourself here."

Anette vanished again, and Jeanne entered her little kingdom with all her might.

21st Century

She stepped down from the trishaw and gazed at the building. It was a high-rise apartment building very close to the sea, and of course, what she had expected it to be. There was a security guard in the lobby, and she could see him well. She took a quick glance at the whole atmosphere and turned back to pay the driver, making sure that she wasn't being followed by anyone. Her eyes were filled with fright.

"Do you need a ride back?" the driver asked.

She thought for a moment before she gave any reply. Did she really want the trishaw to wait till she returned? Was it going to be a lengthy briefing or a short one? She wasn't sure. But the driver needed a quick answer.

"You can go," she confirmed, and the driver didn't waste a moment.

She walked up to the guard, but her approach was very passive. He looked at her questioningly; it was his own form of welcoming. She thought it was a very hostile reception, and it took her back. She was reluctant, yet wonderfully encouraged to make a move.

"I want to go to the fourth block, sixth floor," she casually mentioned.

The guard smiled, making her more uncomfortable. She was acutely cautious about visiting him. She thought that the whole world was watching her. But her fear was something else: an undue enforcement, which frequently troubled her.

"Does he know that you're coming?" the guard asked with a smile.

"Yes."

He took the receiver and buzzed the number. There was a brief dialogue, and he turned back to her.

"You can go," he said.

She walked towards the elevator which was right next to the staircase. The door opened, and she walked in. One side of its wall was a mirror, and she took a look at herself. She thought she looked good in the carefully picked blue and white cotton frock. Her finely tied up hair succeeded in giving an excellent outline to her very clear face. She took a glance at her eyebrows. There was a scratch mark around one; it had happened in the salon the previous day, as she had unexpectedly shaken her head at the cleanse. Of course, she had tried to cover it, but it was showing anyway. The only thing she could do now was to make up her mind and think that it wouldn't be very noticeable.

She looked at the little screen and discovered that she was still passing the third floor. It was a slow elevator, or perhaps she just felt it was. She feared new people would enter, perhaps people in town who knew her, perhaps the very party that should never know where she was heading. She didn't want anyone to find out by any chance that she was visiting him, but she dreaded one unjustified influence. So, it had to be a secret between the host and herself. However, no one entered. It was a straight lift to the sixth level. The door opened, and she walked out.

Finding the fourth apartment was somewhat tricky. None of the doors were numbered, and she didn't want to ring any doorbell. Perhaps a person she knew might open a door and wonder what she was doing there or whom she was visiting. She stopped for a while at the very next door to the elevator; she had a strong instinct that it was his door. Yes, there was no question about it. She walked towards it and placed her finger on the button without waiting another second. The door opened, and a young boy appeared in front of her.

"Come! He's is waiting for you."

His words surprised her. He hadn't even seen her earlier, so how could he be sure that he was talking to the right girl? Well, perhaps he had an instinct, just like her. He opened the door wide, and she could see her company, not very far from the entrance. She walked in. The young boy closed the door and walked all the way to the kitchen. He was his master's cook, cleaner, and upholsterer who did every little job.

Now the boy wasn't in their vicinity. It was only the two of them. And the fewer the company there was, the sweeter.

"Come, sit down!" he said, inviting her to the couch.

She walked towards the couch and sat down, leaving a gap between them. He placed his eyes on her. It was a beautiful view of an ordinary girl. There was no difference between her and most other girls. But sometimes the most distinct and the unexpected sprang from the humblest. He had no knowledge of this simple truth.

"What have you gathered?" he asked.

"Nothing much yet, sir. I thought you'd brief me today."

"I was going to. But today I have to go out soon. I'd have gone earlier, but I postponed it because you were coming."

She felt happy. The professor, the gigantic figure in the performing arts had postponed his own work for an ordinary girl. It was no mistake. He had done it; he had waited for her.

"Sir, can you please describe Thérèse? Is she an evil character?" she asked.

"No, she really falls in love with Colombel, later in the story, but he ignores her."

"So, both Julien and Colombel die at the end?"

"Yes."

She stopped for a while, wondering if such disasters could happen just for the pleasure of one night's love. Of course, she knew that it was possible.

She thought deeper into the story and quickly concluded that Colombel was the main interest of the professor, who was sitting right next to her now. She was prejudiced that a professor of performing arts wouldn't be ready to take up with any other than the nice-looking character. But she was wrong. He was fixed to Julien.

"Sir, this short story was written by Émile Zola, more than a century ago."

"Yes, that's his importance here."

She stopped again, to wonder if it was necessary to find facts about the artist when he really should give importance to the art. What was more important? The art, the artist, or both? She had many questions but didn't spend time answering herself. She was happily driven by the waves of her own pleasure.

"A girl worked in his house as a laundress, a girl who ironed clothes. He ended up having a very close relationship with her; she became his *second wife*," he said.

Her heart was wide open to all his stories about the controversial character from history, and she enthusiastically listened to him. However, neither of them knew that he was wrong in this specific description. Jeanne Rozerot was not a laundress; she was a seamstress. But they were both blind to this simple fact about her.

"How long can you stay here?"

"Not more than another half an hour, sir. I have an afternoon lecture, too."

"I won't keep you long, then."

She stood up to go, and he accompanied her up to the door. They looked at each other many times as they walked to the door, but neither spoke. He looked deep into her, gripping her tiny eyes by his, a wondrous grasp. They both stopped at the door, but she was reluctant to open it. She wanted to be there longer, perhaps to find herself in a lovely conversation, one about a historical controversy or something similar.

He held the door lock and waited awhile.

"When will you come again?"

"When do you want the work done, sir?"

"Take your time, don't think of any limit."

"Okay, sir," she said. "There's something I want to tell you, too."

"What?"

"Just something about me, but I'm not sure if this is the time to say it."

He smiled, taking it lightly, and she was encouraged to carry on with her decision.

"I'll tell you in time, sir."

He nodded his head as if to agree with her, but it left a question in him.

A few long moments passed. He kept watching her face very closely without letting her notice, holding her gently by her shoulder. She became sensitive but made sure that he didn't notice her vulnerability or her negativity. She was successful; he didn't notice a thing. He opened the door and watched her walk into the elevator. She turned around and saw him still standing at the door. His eyes were relaxed on the ordinary charm. Perhaps it was her ordinariness that made her rare. Yes, she was a simple scarcity. It wasn't only he who was blind to it, but she was also as well.

She smiled one last time before the elevator closed, and he returned it. She came down and passed the guard without even giving him a glance. A trishaw was stopped right outside, and she got into it.

19th–20th Century

The sewing room looked like it was built for the same purpose, or at least for something similar. Large and much longer than the average length of a bedroom, it possessed remarkable vitality and most wilfully accepted the pretty lass who walked in.

Jeanne looked around. There were three sewing machines kept distanced from one another, and she understood that there had been more than one seamstress working there. But at present, she knew that it was only her. That was what she had been told. She preferred it that way. If she had been asked to work with more people, she would have adjusted herself to it well enough, but right now it was a different story.

She began to examine the machines. They looked isolated. She wondered if they were of the same brand, but it didn't take her long to identify that they were from three different companies. She carefully placed her hand on one. The little wheel on the upper part of the machine moved slowly with her hand. She quickly held it tight before it turned again. As she turned the pedal, she could tell that it was in excellent condition. She moved to the next machine and continued the same process. It was a success. She understood that all three machines were in excellent condition, so she tried to choose. The one in the far corner picked her eyes just as much as her eyes picked it. It was a mutual choice. She walked towards it to examine it closer.

It was indeed a modern sewing machine. She sat down on the little seat in front of it and started understanding her friend, feeling that she was most welcomed. So, too, felt her friend. They communicated well. It was a friendly, pleasing conversation. She felt that she was found by an anticipated friend. They both understood each other brilliantly well.

She withdrew herself, moved closer to the clothing materials and found a little piece of cloth. Folding it correctly, she walked back to the machine, and her friend accepted it. She sat down, placed it under the needle and pressed the fitting lever down. The pedal started slowly. The little piece of cloth began to move down the line, and the sewing was happening beautifully. She was happy, and so was her friend.

She turned to the fabrics again to find lots of it, all kept together. Of course, there hadn't been a seamstress for some time. This became evident when she saw the loads in wooden racks. Still, she was unclear of one simple fact, and she kept asking herself the same question: Why such a lot of sewing for a little household?

The racks were fixed at a level above her head, so she had to make use of the little stool to reach them. Most of the fabrics were thick, and she felt them with both hands. There were thin ones, too, most probably, for dresses. The thick ones looked like they were suitable for curtains. She stepped down the stool and felt her own dress, made with a thick fabric, then quite suddenly she saw her reflection in the mirror, fixed to the wall.

She felt that she looked much better than she thought. Her blue and white dress was noticeably long, and it shone in the sun, making the whole sewing room much brighter than the rest of the house. Her hair was untidy. She looked as if she just got up from her bed, but it made her look fresh. She walked towards the mirror and fixed her hair, thinking that it would have become messy on her way there. She was right; she had stood outside a long time, considering the decision to take over the sewing of this household, not really knowing that she had been taking time to decide something else.

She turned back to the room again, trying to understand it better. There was a square table, quite a large one with drawers on two sides. She began to examine it. The three metal boxes kept on it, no doubt, had sewing tools in them. She opened each to discover that she was right. There were needles, threads, pins, tapes, and thimbles in them. There was a copper thimble in one of the boxes; it had a design on it. She put it on her finger. It looked like a piece of jewel. Her finger was pretty. A smile appeared on her face as she admired her finger in it, and she quickly put it back in the box.

Her next concern was the broad set of drawers, and she opened one to find reels of yarn in it. Different shades of colours were packed together, and she knew that it wouldn't be hard to find the colour she would want. There was no end to her beautiful discoveries. She turned away from the drawers, stunned by something that idled in a corner. She walked towards it, wondering why she hadn't seen it earlier. It almost swallowed her. She felt that it stood alone, away from everything else in the room. It was a friendly little unfriendliness: an enormous ironing table, and an old electric iron.

She touched the table and the iron with both hands, feeling the comfortable discomfort. They both welcomed her from the future, a very warm welcome. She felt the greeting, although she was unable to fathom the intricacy of the objects. But there was something that they tried to convey. She knew it; yes, she knew it with all her heart.

There were shelves fixed under the face of the table. She bent down to examine them and found that the electric iron on the table wasn't the only one there. Many were kept underneath. She wasn't sure if they worked, and she didn't want to try them, either. But she tried the one on the table, and it was in excellent condition. She was happy. However, the ironing table and the iron left an unanswered puzzle in her.

"Jeanne, madame wants the curtains in her room done, for a start."

Jeanne didn't know that Anette had entered until she heard her. She was staring at the ironing table, and Anette realized that she was puzzled.

"This ironing table is here so that you'll be able to give a good finish to your work. Whatever you make, a dress, curtains, table decorations or whatever they may be, you can complete them by pressing. Nothing will be complete without it," she said.

But she was wrong in reasoning it out. Jeanne had no question about their function. It was something else that troubled her within, something that she didn't understand.

"Come, let's go!" Anette said.

The young seamstress complied with the command, quickly grabbing a toolbox from the table. Anette didn't fail to notice the one she picked. She smiled to herself. She liked the girl very much, not as a seamstress but as a well-organized young worker. In spite of her messy hair, there was something very nice and neat about her.

"I should have shown you madame's room first," Anette said as they came out of the sewing room.

They started walking towards the room. It was the first-ever work Jeanne was assigned to do, and she was getting enthusiastic about it. She was determined to do the best that she could.

Soon they were in Alexandrine's bedroom, and well at work.

"I'll be here until you take measurements. I'm sure you need help," Anette said, standing aside and leaning herself on the wall.

Jeanne kept the box on the dresser, taking out the tape.

"Of course, I need your help," she said, and Anette volunteered.

There was much more work than she had expected. It was a large room with large windows. She unrolled the tape and began her work. Anette helped her whenever she was asked. She was a pleasant woman who knew nothing about needlework. For her, it was all about cooking and kitchen work. But it wasn't all that hard to help the young seamstress when she took measurements for her first bit of work. She knew that the sizes of the windows in Alexandrine's room differed, and for that matter, Jeanne needed more help than expected.

The two were very harmonious in their work. There was no disagreement at any level. It also didn't look like an assigned job. They spontaneously volunteered to do what they did. One of them, however, was different from the other. Anette enjoyed watching Jeanne at work, how her hands moved and how her mind was focused. She admired her, well engrossed in her work. While Jeanne was absorbed in her task, Anette was absorbed in watching her.

"All done," Jeanne said, rolling up the tape and placing it in the box. She put the little notebook and the pencil back and closed the box. "I'll make a move, then," she said as she left the room.

Anette turned to the room to see if there was anything else to be done. There was absolutely nothing, so she walked to the kitchen. By then, Jeanne had already lost herself in her little sewing room, so Anette didn't see her for a long time after that.

Jeanne was the queen of her little kingdom. But no, she was truly the little princess there. She took the little wooden stool and climbed on it. Her eyes moved swiftly, trying to pick the right materials for the curtains. The dull red was the best, and she stopped at it. Her hands were quicker than her mind, so they drew it out and kept it on the table. She thought that the curtains for the windows closer to the bed—the ones with smaller frames—perhaps needed some embroidery, and she started to do the other curtains that required less work, first. And that was the best decision.

She spread the materials on the table and marked down the points with a pencil before she started cutting. It wasn't a difficult task at all. Making curtains was one of the easiest jobs that she had ever done. When she completed cutting them to the right length and width, she took them to the machine and started stitching. As she turned the little wheel with her hand, her right foot was placed on the pedal, and it moved with rhythm to turn the larger wheel at the bottom. It was meant to be systematic, but for her, it was a melody. The machine was producing a sound, but she hardly heard it. She was far away, focusing on the curtains. Soon, she was done with the work.

The curtains were made by lunchtime, and she decided to fix them before Anette came again, letting go of the thought that she might need her help. However, there was something that needed to be done before she took them to the final set up.

It was ironing.

She took them to the ironing table, plugged in the iron and began to spread them on the table while the iron warmed up. Just like sewing, she felt that it was the first-ever time she was ironing. Why was she a stranger to that bit of work? She tried to find a reason for this unfamiliarity. It was a very familiar, beautiful strangeness.

The ironing was done. She didn't fold the curtains as she didn't want any folding lines. The iron in her hand worked beautifully, pressing excellently, and at the end, the curtains had a beautiful finish.

She carried them to Alexandrine's room in a large basket, happy that no one saw her walking back there. Alexandrine was having lunch, and there was no one in her room. It was the ideal time for Jeanne to be engaged in her goal, as everyone else in the household was occupied in their own tasks, not paying attention to her.

Soon she was in the master bedroom. She looked around to find something to climb on, to reach the window frame, but there was nothing of the sort. The only way she could reach it was, climbing up on the table which was kept in the corner of the room, and she took advantage of it. The table wasn't heavy. She pulled it to the right place and climbed onto it. Soon she was done with the very first curtain, and she moved to the other end of it. Done with no delay, she climbed down to admire her work. It was beautiful, truly beautiful. The room almost took the same colour. She was happy. There were yet some more to fix, and she moved to them.

One by one they were getting done, and she was happy that no one entered the room. She hardly noticed the swiftness of time. At the last curtain, she became even more pleased, as she now had only a bit left to do and would be fully done fixing the longer ones. However, little did she know that someone else had just entered the room. How strange that she didn't even notice his grand entrance! It was a little surprise. Was she that absorbed with the curtains? Truly, yes, she was.

He entered to find a young lass doing a beautiful bit of work up on a table. He stopped short at the view. It was something that he had never expected. He wondered who she could be, and then remembered that there was to be a new seamstress in his house. He had never been interested in finding out details of her employment, but he was sure that this was her. He could hardly see her face as she was facing the opposite way, but he was fascinated by the first sight of this appealing young woman.

He didn't move his eyes away from her. Her beautiful form was apparent, especially when she had her hands high up trying to fix the last curtain to the nail. Her slender waist was most eye-catching. He had heard that the new seamstress would be a very young girl, so he knew that he was decades older than her, but right now, that didn't really matter. He watched her with approving eyes and wished by no means to take them away from her. He observed how rhythmically her hands were moving, how eagerly she climbed down and admired her own bit of work and how elegantly her whole figure moved with everything she did. He was amply impressed, not only by the work she was doing but by everything, just everything about her.

He still had his eyes on her as she fixed the last curtain, and he began to admire her hair. It was long, but she had tied it on top, so the length wasn't very clear. He thought it would have been better if she hadn't tied it. She would have looked lovelier with her hair down.

He was lost in his thoughts when he suddenly saw his own reflection in the mirror; he was disappointed at not being a match to her. She most definitely had very youthful choices of her own. He stood where he was and took a deeper look at his reflection. He could see the well-known man of esteem who lived out loud, who respected every opinion but always went ahead with his own. He kept looking at his reflection: the controversial figure in political liberty, the proponent of Naturalism. The man of esteem was falling short in front of a simple, ordinary girl just after seeing her for the very first time. In fact, he still hadn't even seen her face.

Jeanne got down from the table and started admiring her last bit of work. She was happy and content about the first-ever work she had done in the house. She turned to look at the other curtains she had fixed. They looked excellent. The shade gave the whole bedroom a very cozy look. She was happier than words could ever express. Her feet tiptoed backwards as she admired them, not yet aware that there was a stranger in the room. Also, he didn't wish to let her know about his presence there. He just allowed things to happen. Of course, he liked what was about to happen, and he welcomed her with his whole self.

Jeanne was only a few steps ahead of the monsieur, and she ended up backing into him, almost falling down. He helped her to stand up, and she turned around to meet him.

She was worried about what might happen now, but he liked it. He could see her face very well, her bright eyes, black curls, and that very clear face. Jeanne felt very nervous and afraid. She knew she was working for the family of an aristocrat. In fact, this was the first time she was really seeing him.

"Are you okay?" he asked.

She began to tremble. She was extremely nervous. He knew it, and he just enjoyed watching her reaction. He wanted to hold her in his arms but made very sure that he didn't. Jeanne, on the other hand, wanted to disappear from his eyes. In brief, a doe was caught by a lion in the jungle. The only difference was that the lion here, had no intention of hurting the innocent; he simply loved her presence.

"I'm very fine, monsieur," she said, looking down.

He still had a smile on his face. He wanted to draw her closer to him, to take those trembling lips, to have his arms around her slender waist. But it wasn't the time.

"Why are you not facing me?" he asked.

She smiled but had her eyes down. The more he spoke, the more she was nervous. She preferred maintaining silence, and so she did.

"When you work here, I'd rather have you answer my questions," he said firmly, and she was more nervous this time.

"What's your name?" he asked.

"Jeanne. Jeanne Rozerot."

"What are you doing here in this room? Did you get permission to move tables here?"

"Madame wanted the curtains done, so I thought she'd be happy if they were done before she came in."

"You're not allowed to think on your own and do things when you work here. You need to follow instructions! Do you understand?"

"Oui, monsieur."

"Who asked you to pick red?"

"I just thought it was a good colour," Jeanne softly whispered.

There was silence, as it was another unacceptable answer. She was just told that she wasn't allowed to work on her own accord, but she had done so.

"Why are the other windows not done yet?" he asked, turning his eyes towards the smaller windows.

"I thought they needed embroidered curtains," she replied, once again contradicting his commands.

He was silent and so was she, for some time.

"Who asked you to push the table over there?" he asked.

"There was no other way that I could fix the curtains, so I thought that was the best thing to do."

The more she spoke, the more she proved that she was going against his expectations. There were no more questions, anyway. She walked back to the table again and carried it to its original spot, then took a last look at her work, wondering if she had anything else to organize in the room. The room was in good shape, and she wanted to go back to her little *sewing office* now. She wondered if she needed his approval for that. However, she hesitated to make any kind of expression.

Before she left, she had to look at him to find out if he was paying attention. But she was reluctant to raise her head to look at him. Nevertheless, she succeeded in finding out where his eyes were focused, without really looking at him, and started walking to the door with no sound.

"I haven't yet asked you to leave." His deep voice became active again, and she stopped.

This time she was encouraged, with great effort, to raise her head, and she saw his face clearly, for the first time.

Controversial French novelist,
Major figure in political liberty,
Proponent of Naturalism,

She saw the man of esteem who lived out loud, who voiced himself for justice and political liberty. Yes, she could see him very clearly, the proponent of Naturalism: Émile Zola, the forlorn.

"Can I go back to my work, monsieur?" she softly asked.

"Yes, you may," he said, silently smiling to himself.

She slowly walked out of the room without making a sound and rushed to her little sewing room as soon as she could.

21st Century

She sat down in her bedroom trying to decide how her search should begin, her dig into the past, her investigation into the controversy. She was taking her time getting started, anyway, quite unsure if he was from the past or present. Sitting for a long time in front of her computer, her hands tied, her mind lingering regularly on the art, artist, both and neither—she decided in a flash of a moment and began her dig.

Controversial French novelist,
Major figure in political liberty,
Proponent of Naturalism,
I ink my pen to write thyself.

It wasn't her best experience. She passed through several pieces of art from the artist. There were many, and they all consisted of the same theme: human emotions at their highest extremes. She skipped his work for some time to look at him, the man of esteem who lived out loud. Yes, he really lived out loud. There didn't seem to be a time that he didn't express himself and work for what he knew was right; he worked hard for justice. She was moved by all his major works.

She frequently took her eyes off the art while concentrating on the artist. She thought there was something sad about this controversial novelist.

Monsieur Zola thy lonely self,
I witness after those silent years,

Listening to the soft whispers of her heart, she continued her search, completing long hours, wondering if she performed adequately, not knowing that it wasn't at all going to be satisfactory for the present artist, the professor who held hands with the historical controversy.

It was dark outside. She thought she had to make her way to the balcony, so she did. Darkness had done wonders to the sky, glittered with spreads of sparkles. She tried to fathom the vastness of the creations out there as she was able to have a clear view of the sky. She sat down, trying to grasp the universe. It was impossible. She was distracted by some talkativeness. There was a sudden pause, and she began to see the same vastness again. She was far away from her body, walking among the shines. And she could feel nothing but her insignificance.

She came back to herself again, disturbed by a little insect that flew right in front of her face. It was directed to the light bulb, and she had to hurry now. She turned off the light, saving the little life, but didn't know where it flew afterwards. There was a large number of insects fallen down right below the light bulb, and her heart was filled with sympathy.

A plague of insects had been flying to the gleam, knowing nothing about their fate. How unfortunate! They were misled by the beauty of the glow and didn't know where they would end up until they were faced with their tragic fate. She felt sadder looking at the tiny lives, some still struggling, and wondered how they might be feeling. Really, she was extending sympathy for all living beings faced with misery. She blamed herself for not seeing them earlier, as she could only save a single creature, and the others were already gone. But the tiny creature she saved would have been flying towards another blaze, although she didn't know it. The insect would have already fallen by then. How pathetic!

She walked back to her bedroom as the telephone rang and heard the most anticipated voice on the other end. It was him! She was happy to hear him, and his voice held the highest magnetism.

"How far have you done?"

"Quite a long way, sir. But some more to do," she said and remembered a major fact that she thought he missed out. "He died of carbon monoxide poisoning. And it's a suspected murder."

"Yes," he said.

She was disappointed by his brief answer. She thought she was breaking news. But it was no news to him. Anyway, she had to draw his attention somehow, and she knew of one way.

Her mind ran to the past, not so long ago:

On her first day, she had entered the busy campus grounds, rushing herself, preoccupied, almost in another world. That was typical of her. She could be dreamy and float in the air for hours. So, she had been blind to the crowd and the rush hour. She had crossed the narrow lane, hardly noticing the approaching motor vehicle. It had come to a sudden halt, giving a loud sound, bringing her to her proper senses. She had stopped herself with the vehicle, aiming her eyes on the two men who sat in it. One had been the driver, and the other had been her focus of attention now: the professor of performing arts. He had gazed at her, his eyes filled with irritation for this ordinary, everyday student who hadn't stopped for an oncoming vehicle. They both had had their eyes on each other for a quick moment. It had been a narrow escape from a serious car accident, perhaps from a severe injury.

"You don't have a perfect memory, sir," she said.

"What?" he asked, as it was an unexpected comment from an ordinary girl.

"You forgot that we had met earlier."

"We? Met earlier? Where?"

"Try to remember!"

There was a pause. She really had him in suspense. He began to think. He was quite sure that he hadn't met her on a previous occasion. So, the simple, ordinary girl had the great professor in her fervent grip.

"Where on earth did I meet you earlier?" he asked, thinking out loud.

"Try to remember, sir!" she said in her playful tone.

He kept thinking, trying his best to call back any memories of this girl, the student who was posing a simple question on the other end.

"Try some more, sir!" she said.

She spoke in a musical tone, and he was carried away by her liveliness. However, he failed; he could recall nothing. She was happy, although she knew that he was going to remember nothing anyway.

"It happened like this, sir…"

She stepped forward into a long story, and he listened with eagerness. "It happened on my first day on campus. You almost knocked me down by your car and tried to kill me."

The story went on in detail, and he listened, enjoying her liveliness. There was noticeable silence at the end, and it looked like the highly esteemed professor was hit by the words of the simple girl. She took advantage of the silence that prevailed, expressing herself to the maximum extent.

"How could you even think of knocking someone down like that?" she said, continuing with the joy of sweetly accusing him, although her intention was something else. "And you don't even remember. It was my first day on campus. What a terrible thing to happen! Someone told me, another new student, that you were a professor. By then, you had already gone."

She enjoyed the silence on the other end, but he seemed to be well affected by the story she had just related. Suddenly their conversation ended, and she felt bruised, as she knew that the great professor was strongly affected by her random story. His silence was saying it all. So, she spoke again.

"I was just saying it. It's no blame. It's nothing to remember, anyway. Campus is crowded at new entrances," she said, trying to pacify him.

Her words made him talkative this time.

"But I was affected," the esteemed professor replied.

She stopped to listen, but no more words came from the other end. So, she spoke again.

"I was just saying it, to have a good laugh and make you laugh. It's no blame," she said in the same pacifying tone. "By the way, sir, do you remember what I said?"

"Which?"

"That I have something important to tell you?"

"Yes, but you're not saying what it is."

"Sir, you didn't even ask me what it is."

There was a smile on the other end, but she couldn't see it. She had touched his heart with some kind of warmth. It was evident, but neither party really knew it. So, it went on.

The search continued the next day and the day after and the day after that. There didn't seem to be an end to it. However, the same thought haunted her: the importance of the artist and the art. Her understanding was that there was less prestige to the artist when the art was recreated. Perhaps she was right and perhaps wrong. Anyway, now it was time to focus entirely on the art.

She thoroughly studied the art, wondering how distinct it was. She thought that this specific piece of art had a universal appeal. Disasters could rise from an individual attempt to satisfy one night's love. Perhaps, the characters in the story of his choice were universal, just like he expressed.

She looked deeper into the story and began to live in it, with Julien playing the flute—a very old flute, a wooden one. The music spread through the countryside. It was a lovely melody. Anyone would have fallen in love with it, but not as much as Thérèse did. She stood by her window listening to the lovely music played by the unattractive man, totally ignoring him. But he misunderstood her, thinking that she loved him.

Was it not possible, anyway, for a lovely maiden to fall in love with an unappealing man? It was possible. Yes, it was definitely possible. But Thérèse's main interest was Colombel, the young man. It wasn't clear if she really loved him, but the best assumption was that Thérèse didn't love anyone except herself.

The inquisitive writer fell asleep with the three characters, and soon the next day dawned.

By this time, the genius professor who was all set to start his work was listing his own inserts. He sat at his table trying to gather the facts he was drawing in his mind. It wasn't a difficult task. He had his hands and that mastermind, full of work. Suddenly, however, he was disturbed. Something came flying into his window, and he quickly looked over. Seagulls were flying towards the sea, and one of them had knocked on the glass, making a loud sound, but it had fixed itself, flying again. He stood up and walked to the window to find the birds flying far away now, making a design in the sky and changing it from time to time.

The boy was in the kitchen getting things ready for his master's herbal porridge, his favourite breakfast. He made it fine. He went to the front to see where the master was and saw him standing at the window. He didn't want to disturb him, although he knew that it was time for his morning meal. The master didn't know that the boy had come to the front, so he still had his eyes aimed through the window. The boy wondered what he was looking at. He walked closer to him without being noticed and saw that his eyes were aimed far away at the sea. The boy smiled. It was one of the rare times that he found his master in deep thought. He could also see a slight smile on his face.

"Sir!" he called. But he was hardly heard, so he had to call a second time: "Sir, the porridge is ready."

The words took the professor by surprise. He wasn't happy that the boy had come that close to him, to gather what he was doing. He didn't want his worker to see for any reason, his pensive mood.

"Bring it to the table!" the professor ordered.

The boy complied with the instructions, going back to the kitchen. He brought the porridge to the table. It was made with herbs and boiled rice. He stood there while his master had his meal, and began his usual conversation. It was habitual in their routine.

"Sir…"

The boy began to speak, and his superior slightly raised his head but said nothing.

The boy posed his question: "Shall we call her?"

"Who?" his master asked, pretending that he didn't really know whom his worker referred to.

"One who came here a few days ago."

The master himself wanted to call her. But he hesitated.

"We can't call her like that. We need to wait until she calls us," he said, recalling her request.

Professor was right in his reply. She had asked him not to call her often, under any circumstances. He tried to understand why she had asked this; he hadn't asked her for a reason for this request, nor had she told him. But he was very sure that there was something concealed, something that she wasn't telling him. She had mentioned on several occasions that she had something important to tell him, but she hadn't told him what it was. However, he longed for her visits. What a wonderful theory! The boy wanted to ask him why he didn't want to take the initiative, but he decided not to question him, so he came to his own conclusions about it. He knew his master best. Well, he knew that his master never did anything to hurt his self-esteem, and he thought that taking the initiative to call her would bring him down. The boy enjoyed this situation anyway.

"Sir,"

He spoke again, while the superior was continuing with his meal, listening to him.

"Shall we buy a little gift for her?" the boy suggested.

"Like what?"

The professor became interested, and the boy knew that he made the right suggestion, so he made use of the opportunity.

"Perhaps we could send her a *thank you card*."

Well, this was a brilliant idea coming from his worker. But he was silent. He decided to go ahead with it. Just then, the telephone rang, and the boy picked it up. He identified the voice on the other end, and he was happy.

"Sir, she's calling you."

By this time, the professor had already eaten his breakfast and was standing up. He decided to answer her from the extension in his bedroom.

"Ask her to hold for a while!" he said.

He walked all the way to his bed and picked up the receiver, overcome by a certain level of annoyance, as she was late to call him.

"Why are you calling now?" he asked.

She understood his irritation and promptly woke her voice.

"I'm almost done with the work, sir," she said.

There was calmness in her voice, but he spoke with the same irritation.

"You know very well that I'm waiting for the work. Is it all done now?"

"Yes, sir," she said.

She was disturbed by his tone and didn't really know any reason for his irritation. She didn't even know that she was expected to contact him much earlier. He was silent, but she held the receiver until he spoke.

"I've been waiting to hear from you. Why have you taken so long?"

She remained silent, and he could picture the face of the girl. He was beginning to understand her. She looked up at him with awe, full of admiration. He knew it with all his heart. He enjoyed the silence on the other end, but at the same time, he didn't enjoy it at all. There had to be an end to it, so he asked his question.

"When are you coming here next?"

The simple, ordinary girl stopped at his question. She knew that she couldn't wander in her silence anymore. She had to be prompt.

"Maybe next week," she said.

"Which day? Wednesday afternoon is my free time," he said.

She knew that she couldn't make it on Wednesday, but she didn't mention it. She was just enduring his request. Why? She didn't understand the reason. So, their conversation ended with the highly esteemed professor believing that she was going to visit him on the day he mentioned.

She walked to the kitchen for a glass of water and couldn't help noticing a tiny ant in the jug. Yes, a tiny ant was drowning in water. Her heart was filled with sympathy towards the little life in struggle. She quickly took it out, and happily watched it moving, on her finger.

By this time, over on his end, he was working. With swift memories of his childhood, he was drawing his art in his mind:

There had been an old man living in his hometown, who had spent the evenings sitting under a tree, playing the flute. One day, coming home after school, the young child had stopped at the flutist. Attracted to the soft melody, he had walked towards him. The old man playing the instrument had hardly noticed the child who had stood there for a very long time, touched by the melancholy tune.

He could still hear the music from his childhood when he was in his own lonely atmosphere. He quickly brought his mind back to the present, trying to recall the melody. It wasn't difficult to place the old musician in Julien. That was his best decision. Yes, he fit there well.

By this time, she was in her little bedroom dreaming, the controversial historical character, Émile Zola, haunting her. She thought it was best to find out more about him, so she began.

He could be seen standing there in his room near his window. It was early morning, and he was watching the beautiful sparrows. They sang a beautiful song, but he hardly heard it. She watched him much more closely. He didn't look happy. In fact, he looked sad. The morning brought him some kind of expectation. Was it the young seamstress that he longed to see? Yes, he waited for her, but he hadn't identified this to be true.

His window faced the front yard of the house, and suddenly he saw a tiny figure advancing. He observed her. Yes, it was her! The beautiful dressmaker! He was happy. He felt that his day was complete. He watched as she walked to the main entrance; as the tiny figure became larger, he was able to see her clearly. His eyes were filled with admiration. He was completely taken with her graceful walk. The long blue dress she wore was in harmony with everything about her. He watched her, trying to understand what difference she would make. He wondered why he thought that she would make a difference. But he was very sure that she would.

Unaware of her admirer, Jeanne hurried her feet as she was already late, and found herself in front of the main entrance. His ears pricked up to listen to her beautiful entrance. It was taking longer than usual. He wanted to walk up to the door, but he was reluctant; it could arouse suspicion. He thought it was the longest time in the world. Still, he could hear nothing.

She stood there rubbing the mud off her boots before she knocked on the door, not knowing that her highly esteemed superior was waiting for her.

19th–20th Century

She was taking a long time to rub the dirt off her boots, and the long wait was building curiosity in her lover. The thought of going to the door came over him many times, but he silenced it.

And at last, he heard the entrance of the little allure.

Jeanne placed her boots on the rack and hung her coat. Anette waited until she was done and accompanied her to the little *sewing office.*

"Madame wants one of her dresses started today," Anette informed her. "Which one?"

"I'm not sure. I think it's the green one."

Jeanne tried to remember the pattern assigned for the green. It wasn't a difficult one. Nothing was difficult for her, anyway, where any type of needlework was concerned. She mastered it.

She entered the sewing room, and Anette left her. She took a glance at the room, scanning it with her sharp eyes. It was neat. It was perhaps the tidiest place in the whole world. She walked up to the rack where the fabrics were arranged and took the green velvet to her hand. It was lovely. She felt it with both hands, trying to understand how well it would suit Alexandrine. Well, the design surely went very well with the velvet.

She continued to feel it, knowing from the bottom of her heart that it would never suit her simple self. She turned pages of the pattern book until she reached the right one. The block was right there, but she wasn't happy with it. She needed her own block, one she trusted, and she had to meet Alexandrine to request a time to take measurements. Her best guess was that she was in the living room, seated by the fire.

Soon she was there, very close to Alexandrine, but she still couldn't see her face. Alexandrine had turned all the way to the opposite direction, and her eyes were aimed out of the window at far eternity. She didn't notice the entrance of the young girl. Jeanne stood there, for the lady to see her. But it didn't look like it would happen, so she spoke.

"Madame…"

Jeanne waited awhile to receive a response, then realized that she had to address her again.

"Madame!"

This time she was louder, and so she was heard.

"Yes?"

"I need to do a new block."

"Sure."

"If I can have time for measurements…" Jeanne stopped with no proper end to her request.

"I see. I'm impressed. You want to work on your own block."

Jeanne felt happy about being understood.

"You can go back to the sewing room. I'll call you when I'm ready," Alexandrine said.

Jeanne hurried back, not knowing that she was being watched by her lover, the lover that she never knew existed.

The monsieur, the man of esteem, had watched the young lass walking to the living room and then back to her sewing room. He had heard the conversation between the two to some extent, so he knew that Jeanne was expected to wait until she was called by Alexandrine. Jeanne entered her *little office* quickly, and the monsieur watched her from another angle.

She got lost in herself.

She was struck by a wonderful idea. It was a good time, as she knew that Alexandrine was going to take awhile to call her. She decided to draft her own patterns and took some blank papers to the table. The pencils were in the drawer, and she made use of them. It took awhile, but it came out beautifully. She wondered if the pattern would suit Alexandrine and concluded that it would suit no one else better than herself. She held the paper in her hand at a distance from her eyes, admiring its beauty, and ended up doing another, then another and another.

The dominant figure who was a wonderful lover still watched her. It was splendid. He watched when the pencil lost itself in her lovely grip, and the draft began. He thought there was music as the pencil moved in her hand, on the paper. Everything happened to a rhythm. An untouched smile was planted on her face in admiration, whenever the paper was held in her hand at a distance.

What a pretty lass in the form of a seamstress, working in his own house! He couldn't take his eyes away from her, so he waited until they did it by themselves, but they were stubborn. Suddenly, the lovely seamstress rose to her feet, taking the monsieur by surprise. It was unexpected. He thought he should move away, but things were happening quickly. Anette's voice echoed in the hallway. She was coming to the sewing room. The monsieur hurried his feet, as he definitely had to move away before he was seen by either of them. His self-esteem didn't want to face any encounter.

"Jeanne, madame's waiting for you," Anette said loudly, as she stepped towards the sewing room.

The monsieur's face turned completely to another mood. He met Anette face to face in the hallway. The servant hadn't expected to run into him on her way, so the unexpected meeting made her come to an abrupt stop. She moved to a side, giving space to his majestic self. He passed her without even giving her a glance.

Anette entered the sewing room and saw that Jeanne was ready with her toolbox to meet Alexandrine, to take her measurements for the block.

"Ready?" she asked.

"Yes," Jeanne said, leaving the room with everything she needed for the duty.

She soon found herself with Alexandrine, who was waiting for her. The twosome looked at each other, smiled, and began the work. One was busy taking measurements while the other cooperated. Bust, waist, hip, arm, and neck were completed in sequence, and then the grand entrance took place.

The silent lover walked straight towards the little bedside table, opened its drawer and went through the papers inside. It almost looked like he was trying to find something, although he absolutely had no reason to be there at that time. He was very subtle; he could make it look like he was fully focused on what his hands were doing when he actually wasn't. His eyes were nowhere else but on the beautiful seamstress.

He watched her as she took measurements. The tape was unrolled in her hands and sent everywhere she wanted. How harmoniously everything happened! He couldn't help but admire her beautiful waist. He was a student of it.

"Madame, can you stretch your arms now?"

"It's time for your neck."

"The front waist."

"The back waist."

"Hip."

Jeanne used her words only at the right time. What a lot of music he found in them! He couldn't leave the room. But he had to. In a quick second, he made his move and left the room. Jeanne was done with her work soon after, so she went to the sewing room and started working on the block.

The monsieur was in the library, losing himself in his masterpiece, wondering why it disturbed him many years after it was published. Perhaps he was making it ready for a professor from the future. He was reading it, anyway.

Julien had learned the flute alone. For a long time, an old yellow wooden flute from a bric-a-brac dealer in the Place du Marche had remained one of his greediest desires. He had the money, but he dared not go in, to buy it for fear of being ridiculous. Finally, one evening, he was emboldened to carry the flute, running with it tight against his chest, hidden under his coat. Then, doors and windows closed, very softly so that it wasn't heard, he had practised an old method for two years, one he found in a small bookseller. For six months only, he ventured to play the open crossings.

He remembered his character creation, Julien, a difficult task with lots of description, more than Colombel or any other character involved. To have Thérèse come into the scene with Julien, gave importance to him by her role. It was a difficult problem—describing an innocent man's dreadful turn, committing the most unexpected, just for one night's love, as a result of being a victim of love.

He let his mind run to the past and suddenly stopped as the young seamstress entered his mind again. He wondered how enchanting it would have been, if she had really come there, making a beautiful entrance. He pictured her, standing right there in front of him, and himself being her lover and the lover of everything about her. He looked at his reflection in the mirror. How unattractive he looked! How could he ever entice a beautiful young girl? It was impossible. He was sure that she had made her own choices. She could surely choose for herself, and he wouldn't even be her last choice. The more he saw his structure in the mirror, the more his misery rose. He returned to his memories and worked much faster than before, finding himself with the story again.

Julien played the flute every day for beautiful Thérèse de Marsanne, gazing at her in her window. How sad he would have been when the girl didn't even look at him! How dejected and disappointed he would have felt when she totally ignored him although she loved his music! And what an innocent gentleman he was! He never stopped playing for her, even in those circumstances. How delighted he would have been when the very same girl who ridiculed him called him into her bedroom one day! The innocent soul would definitely have thought that she was in love with him.

The esteemed artist felt sad about his own creation. He saw himself in Julien. How surprising! He felt he was failing. He wondered how obliging innocent Julien would have been to commit a crime, just for one night's love. Was it the impermanent, ephemeral human mind that he tried to expose? Yes, perhaps, it was his main concern. The most innocent man on earth, Julien, who even sighed at his dog's grave every day, could swiftly change himself and commit that disastrous act of crime!

The great artist stopped for a while, wondering if it would have been his plight, too, if a young lass had shown him a certain level of love. Would a pretty lass just use him and exploit him, in the pretence of returning the kind of love that he had in his heart for her? He had no answer.

Just then, Anette came to the door with her usual invitation. It was that time of the day.

"Lunch is ready, monsieur."

"I'll be there soon."

He spoke without raising his head, and the servant began to walk back but stopped again at his voice.

"What's for lunch today?"

"Casserole and your favourite Niçoise Salad."

Anette was surprised. It was, in fact, the very first time that he had a question about a meal. Why was he so concerned about food all of a sudden? It was probably another random question and didn't really mean anything except the words it consisted of. Anette could think of many reasons for his concern about food. She thought of all the reasons in the world, except the real one.

Right in front of her, the monsieur, the gigantic figure in political liberty, the founder of Naturalism, the great artist was, to the best of his efforts, figuring out how he had to change his diet to gain a better physic so that he could look more attractive to an ordinary seamstress. Perhaps he could reduce starch and eat more vegetables and fruit.

He was also trying to think of other methods he could apply, to reach his goal. And then he got a brilliant idea. There was something he could do, to improve his muscles while sticking to a strict diet. He stood up at the thought, and Anette drew back. The monsieur was in very high spirits. She saw eagerness in his face, to a very high extent, something that she had never seen before. The monsieur, too, noticed his own change, and he knew that it was definitely noticeable to anyone around him. He knew that he merged with his own thoughts about the beautiful girl. He was exhibiting all possible reactions of being in love with her, although it was only felt deeply within. It was a one-sided love, well, for the time being. However, he was concerned about the fact that Anette could see his behaviour, as he was lost in his own feelings of love. So, he quickly came back to his grave looks.

"Madame is waiting for you, monsieur," Anette said before she disappeared behind the door.

He came back to his memory for a short time, still wondering what he could be answerable to, for just one night's love, with a young seamstress.

With the same question in his heart, he quickly stood up, not really comprehending his movements. It was very mechanical. He walked towards the mirror to take a deeper look at himself. There was nothing but his reflection. He tried to pull the image out of the mirror. He thought it was just him, with the largely grown waistline, grown with his fame. Yes, he thought it was him, not his reflection.

He carried his large form to the dining table where his wife waited for him. No dialogue took place between them for some time. They ate together, hardly even looking at each other. However, there was something that Alexandrine noticed, something that she couldn't be silent about. She took time to mention it, anyway. She had to observe it for some time before she was sure about it. And even after seeing it, she wasn't sure if it was the right thing to turn into words. So, she silently observed the very noticeable change in her dining partner, until finally, she gave up her silence.

"You're eating only vegetables today."

At this comment, his great self-esteem was shaken. He didn't want anyone to know about his change. It was something he tried to hide from the entire world, giving a blind eye to the natural law, and of course, knowing well that the very attempt to keep things hidden from the world, exposed them. Sometimes such things were discussed centuries later. So, he gave his best effort to continue to conceal his sentiments, not knowing that a professor of performing arts and a girl who wrote had their eyes on him.

"Oh, no, no, no! I eat casserole, too," he said, serving the casserole for the first time.

Alexandrine was stunned by his nervousness. It was one of the rare times that he showed such uneasiness, and she, who knew him best, couldn't help but write it down in her heart. Meanwhile, the monsieur continued to have his meal trying to look as normal as he could.

Lunch was eaten much earlier than usual, and he returned to his office, back to Thérèse, Julien, and Colombel. What a lovely trio! And why was he reading his own masterpiece after so many years?

For five years, Julien lived in the Place des Quatre-Femmes, when, one evening in July, an event upset his existence. The night was very hot, all lit up with stars. He played the flute without light but with a distracted lip, slowing down the rhythm and falling asleep on certain sounds, when all of a sudden, a window of the Marsanne opened in front of him and remained gaping, brightly lit in the dark facade. A girl had come out, and she remained there. She cut out her slim figure, raised her head as if to listen. Julien, trembling, had stopped playing. He couldn't distinguish the face of the girl, he saw only the flow of her hair, already loosened on her neck. And a light voice came to him in the midst of silence.

The monsieur still kept living through Julien, obsessed with his own creation. Sometimes he thought that Julien wasn't a mere creation, but himself. He was gradually inserting himself into Julien. How fascinated Julien would have been to believe that a young beauty was in love with him when he was overwhelmed by his own unattractiveness! Colombel wasn't given much attention. True, he was the lover, but Julien was the remarkable one. He wondered if Thérèse really loved both of them, or if she was making the most out of all situations. Would any other female, placed in the same circumstances, behave in the same way she did? He thought it so; yes, anybody would.

Meanwhile, further away from his office, Jeanne was busy making the dress for Alexandrine. She thought it was gradually becoming very beautiful. However, she had lots to do, to complete it. Suddenly, she had to stop her work as she was called for lunch. She stood up and made her way.

There was quite a long distance from her little sewing room to the dining table. She knew very well that she couldn't complete the dress that day. It was going to take a few more days, but she didn't want it to be even slightly delayed. Specifically, she didn't want to delay any work done by her own hands. She tried to make the maximum of every minute she had, so she hurried, speeding up the little steps she took.

She passed the main area and entered the corridor which led to the rear of the house, meeting her silent lover face to face. It was a coincidental meeting, although he didn't regret it. In fact, he was overjoyed. But Jeanne was alarmed. She began to feel the same nervousness once again. The whole house was silent and, although there were people, she felt that there were only the two of them. She looked at him as he stood right in front of her, giving her a smile, an endearing smile. She wondered why she stopped there without making the slightest attempt to move. Could it have been her nervousness that kept her standing still? Or did she also love this brief meeting?

There was a very brief time of silence, and Jeanne decided to move forward. She attempted, but she was stopped. It wasn't clear if she was deliberately barred from moving forward or if it was her own decision. There was enough space to move even if there was someone right in front of her. Anyway, the result was the same. She couldn't move.

The monsieur had his eyes on the gentle charm. It appeared like he was completely taken with the seamstress, but she didn't know it. She was thinking the opposite.

His eyes were still on her face. He was charmed by her bright eyes, and he lived in them. Her black hair with its bountiful locks cascaded as far as her waist, inviting him. He wanted to take them with both his hands, although he never made a move. He stayed away from her, far away, even though he was near her. There was pin drop silence—they could both hear their heartbeats. And then he broke it, as he couldn't take it anymore.

"So, what have you been doing today?"

"Madame's dress."

"And how do you find work?"

"Everything's good, monsieur."

"Do you know that your job isn't only dressmaking?"

At this question, Jeanne was silent. She knew absolutely nothing about any other job she was assigned with. But she was afraid to give a negative answer.

"Yes."

"So, what else do you have to do?"

Jeanne's mind wandered around her little *sewing office* for some time until she suddenly stopped at something. She quickly woke her voice.

"Ironing and pressing."

"Wonderful."

The dominant monsieur was feeling very gentle inside. He was enduring everything about her. It wasn't easy to stay silent. He confirmed his title: he was her lover, admirer, and devotee. His hands moved softly to feel her hair in admiration. She stood there, unable to move, and not wanting to move, anyway. She wanted to give her whole self to him and not question him or herself about it. But she resisted with her entire self. He softly lifted her face, which had fallen down, and started admiring it again. He was happy when he knew, in a glimpse, that the girl liked him. She loved him, but something was drawing her back. How strange!

She knew it was time to move forward and gave her maximum attempt to it, but it was impossible.

21st Century

She looked down again, trying to withdraw herself, but he understood her appeal and never wanted to let go. He admired her lips; they were trembling in anticipation, and he tried to reach them, but she avoided him with an easy effort.

"Why do you look so scared?" he asked.

She was silent. Far away, she could see the young dressmaker's eyes on her. They looked closely at each other and smiled from a century apart. It was a serene smile, neither of them really identified. She was leaning on the door, and he became very gentle.

"You're trembling," he said.

It almost looked like he enjoyed watching her behaviour. She was a simple, ordinary girl, the most modest girl in the world, and that was her exceptionality, her speciality. It made her distinct. That was what he admired and relished, but he didn't know it.

She recalled the passing moments:

He had asked her why she feared visiting him. The answer had been, of course, obvious.

"Now look at you, sir! You're just yourself. And I'm myself. Isn't it very obvious?"

She was perhaps right. Nevertheless, in addition to the social barriers and expectations that she had to abide by, she was also in danger, and she hadn't told him about it. It was an undue enforcement, which she was still on the brim of revealing. She was undecided about divulging her identity. She feared the leader of a current political party, opposition to the professor's. Going through all the walls wasn't the easiest thing. But she did it, and nothing could stop her.

And she had gone on explaining.

"Sir, I used to think that a professor of performing arts was someone who had a good knowledge of all life situations 'cause they deal with many plots," she had said in the same cheerful tone.

"Yes," he had agreed.

He had stood at a distance, giving a concentrated ear to her. She had just mentioned a sure prospect about his first love: the performing arts, and he had admired it more than anything. So, he had agreed with her description, waiting for the rest of it.

"But sir, you…, you don't seem like you understand anything," she had concluded with an anti-climax, having the same smile on her face.

Her opinion had sweetly hurt his dominant self. He had swiftly made his way to reach her, sweetly annoyed, but taking it as a positive note. However, in steps, he had changed his mind about it.

Her mind ran back to the present.

He held her by her light shoulders and stopped there for a long time. It was the longest time taken in the history of the world. His hands were tender on her, and she rested herself in his arms. He tried several times to reach those lips, still trembling in anticipation. He adored them as much as he was charmed by her uncomplicatedness. Well, perhaps he was misled. He never identified the complicated uncomplicatedness or the negative positivity. Perhaps it was his misfortune and her misfortune, too, which was directed to some kind of fortune. However, they were lovers of coincidence. There was no question about it.

He remembered the girl's readiness to leave his home, but he wished she stayed. At the very thought, the words slipped out his mouth.

"Do you really have to go now?"

She nodded her head, although she, too, wished the opposite.

"Stay with me! There's no hurry to go now." It was a genuine request.

"I'm getting late, sir," she said.

She felt there was no escape for her anywhere, from this beautiful encirclement. She couldn't stop herself from falling into it. It was that charming and enthralling, and she was obsessed. But she drew back in a panic.

"Do you really have to go?" he asked again.

She looked at his face; it was full of expectation. He truly longed for her. He dwelt in solitude. Nothing and no one could lift him from there. His mind was sometimes a wound which never healed. There were reasons for it. Whatever they were, the simple, ordinary girl who was just an acquaintance seemed to be meeting his solitude face to face. She was having a conference with his loneliness. So, he never wanted her to leave. He drew her closer and embraced her again, and she got lost in his arms, forgetting any other existence.

Suddenly, there was a knock on the door, and they were alarmed. The girl went back to the table and started writing again while he stayed at the door. He looked through the peephole and identified the person outside. It was the boy, returning home from town. He had left in the morning to buy some necessities for the kitchen and was standing at the door with a bag full of groceries. The scene relieved his master. Was he panicked at the knock, thinking that it was someone else? Did he fear social barriers, too? Or was it just an unidentified fear?

The boy walked straight into the kitchen, while the master went to the table. It was quite unexpected that she was there visiting his master at this time, so the young boy stopped for a quick moment when he passed her. She raised her head to look at him and realized that he, too, had his gaze on her. They gave each other a quick smile. He was happy that she was there. He envied her visits. Nevertheless, he moved away, stepping towards the kitchen before his master went to the table. She could see the tropical vegetables in his basket and wondered how the professor liked them cooked.

The professor sat at the table. Now she had to change her mind about leaving. They both knew that she had to stay longer, and he began to dictate.

"He was a man of ego who had high regard for every opinion, but always worked with his own."

She wrote down his words, trying to visualize the historical Zola. She could see him clearly now, much better than before. The identification happened while the listener, the writer, was writing down every word dictated by the professor. It was a marvel. He, the most dominant man on earth, had no idea of it. He never knew that he was describing himself in the shade of describing the controversial novelist, Émile Zola. So, he continued with no effort.

"He was a man who lived in the extreme depths of loneliness, so he began a relationship with a laundress who worked in his house just to overcome his sorrows."

She was stunned by his words and slowly lifted her head to look at him. She saw the misery of a solitary man expressing himself on the pretence of describing a controversial historical character he had coincidentally come across while making his art. What a marvellous finding! It was the best discovery ever, but he never knew that he was making it. She, too, didn't realize that she wrote her own story, facing his spoken test. She felt sad for a man who was overwhelmed by his own loneliness that was completely overtaking him. He was rapt in its expanded claws. It was a sea, and he was drowning in it. She could see it clearly. She was effortlessly speaking to it and setting it down on paper.

He continued his dictation.

"In making Julien's character, I remembered a man who lived in my hometown. He used to play the flute every evening. I included his behaviour in Julien."

She kept writing, fact by fact, extending her heart towards his words.

"Also, I strongly feel that Zola, too, included himself in Julien; Julien is a corresponding character."

She instantly looked at the professor, engrossed in his description of Julien. She knew that he was more attracted to Julien than to any other character in the story.

"The story has a universal effect; that's why I have eliminated any particular setting. Also, the three main characters are universal, so I didn't give them names. The story can happen anytime, anywhere in the world."

She wondered if his description of the story was right. Really, it was the truth about any story. All stories had the tendency to happen anywhere in the world, and he didn't realize it. However, she didn't wish to state her opinion. She knew that he would appreciate her opinion but would go ahead with his own.

"I'm sure Zola was referring to impermanence as described in the supreme wisdom of the incomparable, when he was describing Julien's swift turn from the innocent to the wicked, just for one night's love. Julien was an innocent, sympathetic man who cried at his dog's grave every day, but when provoked, he could commit this crime."

Her heart became wide open to his evaluation, and she continued to listen.

"I'm going to the mountains next week, and you'll have enough time to complete it," he said.

He concluded with very high hopes for his amazing recreation of *Pour Une Nuit D'Amour*. He was diving into the making of it, giving it his utmost effort. She was happy that she was part of it now, and that he trusted her with everything she did. He turned to the kitchen and called the boy, who hurried towards the master at his call.

"Yes, sir?"

"Take this lady down the stairs!"

She stood up from her seat and left with the boy, who was happy to have some time with the adorable girl. He loved her and her visits. Sometimes, he wished she could live there. It was a very innocently felt wish, and he adored it.

They called the elevator and walked into it. The boy became very protective over his master's friend. He looked at her face while the elevator was going down. He admired her clear face and liked the way her hair was tied. Her dull blue outfit brilliantly matched her complexion. His eyes drifted down, noticing an unfastened button close to her neck, at the very top. He thought she had to be informed about it.

"Your button!" he said, pointing his eyes towards it.

She looked down, trying to figure out what the boy tried to indicate, and saw that the unfastened button, caught by the strap of her backpack had ended up pulling the collar backwards. It resulted in the exposure of her long neck. She saw it but didn't want to fix it. She wasn't happy that he had pointed it out, so she ignored it. However, her reaction didn't stop him.

"Your button!" he said again.

This time he was being overprotective and spoke in a commanding tone, so she ended up fastening the button. The pair walked out of the elevator and stood in the open lobby. She stopped there as if she saw something she feared.

"What happened? Why did you stop?" he asked.

"Please go and see if there's a black pickup parked out there."

The boy hurried. He didn't know the reason for the girl's fear or doubt. But he walked all the way out of the building and came back.

"There's no pickup there," he said.

He was happy that she was safe, but the reason for her fear wasn't revealed, and he didn't question her about it, either. They both walked out together. There were some trishaws parked on the other side of the road. He knew that she could hire one of them, but he didn't want to call one. He couldn't fall into any type of conversation with her when she was inside, as she was his master's sweet writer, author, and journalist. So, this was the time, but she had to leave. He was sorry. His eyes rested on the trishaws, but he didn't call them. She understood his intention and felt the same. She wished she could stay longer. But they both called one at the same time, and it came over.

"Where to?" the driver asked.

"Just to the town," she said.

She stepped in and looked at the boy, who stood outside now. He was sending her off, although he didn't want to. They looked at each other and smiled. And then she was gone.

She arrived at her destination long before she thought she would and walked into her little home, where a significant pair from history was longing for her. One controversial figure in political liberty and a simple seamstress. They welcomed her at her own home, and she felt comfortable. She fell asleep with them before she even closed her eyes. Sometimes, a deep slumber was the loveliest, and that night, nothing was better. It was a stunningly beautiful voyage to dominant Émile Zola and tender Jeanne.

The next morning, in the library, another pretty little writing started its move while she was digging. Some words were haunting her mind, and her fingers, pencil, and paper were making a lovely chain. She pictured Thérèse, Julien, and Colombel in her mind. Together with her hand, her mind was fully at work, along with Émile Zola and Jeanne Rozerot, of course.

Her mind was a screen with Julien, Colombel, and Thérèse:

How effective was it, if it was said that man was the stronger sex and woman, the weaker? No, it couldn't be right. There lived a woman who proved the opposite. Although her real name was Thérèse, she was a universal character. She made use of every one of the so-called stronger sex and was the winner, always. At a crucial time, to defend herself, innocent Julien was used by her, to dispose of Colombel's body, as she assumed that she had accidentally killed him. During the second climax of the story, on his way to the lake by night with Colombel's body, Colombel, up from his sleep, made clear to Julien that he wasn't killed. Julien and Colombel faced death at the peak of their fight, falling into the lake.

The little writer was in solid contact with her pencil and paper for a very long time. By afternoon she had completed most of it, ending up with an excellent piece of writing. She sympathized with Thérèse, the only one who knew the truth about what really happened to Colombel and Julien. Her own sympathy made her wind up with the finest words.

Who suffers at the end? The dead or the living? The suffering of the dead ends and the suffering of the living continues, just like it happened, Once Upon A Time...

With the best conclusion found, she was done. She knew he would be there anytime, so she waited. It was a long wait, but she stuck it out.

She aimed her eyes again on the screen, and there appeared a man—a man who fought for justice, a man who lived out loud. He was indeed trying to convey a message to her. She looked straight into his eyes, his eyes that were pleading with her. He looked helpless. And far away, she could see the lovely three: Julien, Colombel and Thérèse de Marsanne. She brought her eyes closer to the screen to grasp the truth, drawing back at specific intervals. Wherever she was, the result was the same: *Pour Une Nuit D'Amour* had a different direction. She understood it. It wasn't the story that it ended up being. Her eyes drew back from the screen for a quick second, letting this wonderful piece of history act on its own free will and, of course, in the right way. In a while, the controversy disappeared, and she was alarmed. It was only Julien, Colombel and pretty Thérèse now. They were regretting their own hyperbole.

It was heartbreaking, and she had to hurry. She had to communicate to the professor, the misconception he was in, he who was drawing his art, derived from it.

She wanted to call him, although she was reluctant. Reluctance was something that she struggled with. She didn't think it necessary. These were two conflicting sentiments. She wanted to be rational with him when she conveyed her finding, but it was impossible. She couldn't pretend rationality when she appeared to be irrational. But she wanted to hide behind rationality. She sympathized in love, but nothing could come to the surface. She had to hide everything behind the level-headed girl who was always merry and happy-go-lucky and convey the striking discovery to him.

She decided in a moment of panic as he had to be reached by a sensible voice, so her dreaminess had to be hidden. She took the phone in her hand to listen to the most longed-for voice. And he picked the phone up to hear the most understanding voice.

She began with extreme pretence. It wasn't her; it was someone else.

"Sir, this story is… Let me explain it to you … it's something else. It's not what you think. Do you seriously think that Thérèse did it? No, it happened like this… That night…"

She tried to sound normal, but he didn't enjoy her talkativeness. He didn't know that he was listening to the girl who understood his inner self, more than anyone else. He didn't know that it was her pretended self that was talkative, but she was really trying to say something, a solid discovery, in fact.

"Stories, stories and stories," he said, annoyed.

His tone made her withdraw herself, knowing very well that she was in a futile effort to reveal the truth to him. Actually, there was a reason for her effort, a reason that she didn't understand but tried to unravel. However, he silenced her. And it was he who spoke now.

He went on endlessly, describing Thérèse, Julien, and Colombel. The more he spoke, the more she was silent. She was in her best efforts to understand him, mingled with the same unsuccessful effort to convey her discovery to him. There was no end to his fallacy, and there was no end to her sympathy. They both rose equally and didn't diminish. It was magnificent. At the end of it, his fallacy and her sympathy were reaching eternity.

No matter how much she tried, she never understood that her pure effort to be someone else had discouraged him. For him, she was nothing but just a simple, ordinary girl. There was ordinariness all over this simple girl, and his vacant eyes could see nothing else. Unfortunately, the same deterrence successfully covered the truth about his first direction. How could she understand how much he enjoyed her ordinariness when he didn't? He hadn't enjoyed her pretence. The dominant professor didn't know that he was a devotee of her ordinariness. Both parties didn't know where they really stood. She was disappointed and disheartened, and so was he. He turned back to his work with the same mindset, and she returned home.

It was raining, and she began to watch the beauty outside, through her window. There was something beautiful about the rain, beauty mingled with sorrow. She couldn't see further than the trees that covered her view. If she had gone to the balcony, she would have been able to see the sky, but from the window of the living room, it wasn't possible. The balcony wasn't her favourite place on rainy days, anyway. She preferred to stay cozy inside. She felt as if the rain was taking her somewhere far away, to a long-ago past. She couldn't comprehend it, nor did she try to.

The rain effortlessly took her to the professor's dwelling, and she couldn't stop it. She envied the wonderful getaway. In spite of her dismay, there was a smile on her face. Did she enjoy being that uncomplicated girl? She absolutely did. She wanted to maintain her ordinariness in his eyes and was never a victim of it, as she never wanted to be anything else.

She listened to the weather forecast and learned that the ongoing rain would triumph for a long time, resulting in heavy floods. The area around his home was going to be most affected. The weather alerts about flooding reminded her of her own failure to communicate her finding to the professor. But there was nothing she could do about it. He was just not letting her. She got a brilliant idea. Perhaps she could convey this simple truth to him through the young boy who worked there. Yes, that was the best.

Her eyes were focused far away through the window again. The rain was still falling down. It was gradually becoming heavier, and she liked it.

19th–20th Century

The wind was blowing hard, and it gave a drastic change to the rain. It was freezing cold, but cozy inside.

"I have to go now, monsieur. Someone might…," the young seamstress whispered.

"No one will come here now," he said.

He was holding her face with both hands, trying to reach her lips, but she continued to avoid him, not sure if she really wanted to. He knew it and admired it. At one point, her elusion ended, and they stood there for a long time in each other's arms before he let her go.

"Don't tremble on your way!" he said, admiring the young innocence.

She was flattered, and she hurried herself to the dining table. Food was served, and she started to eat, the beautiful moments lingering in her mind. Her eyes were aimed far away, through the window. The rain was still falling down, but she couldn't understand it. She saw the rain, but she was far away from it. She was charmed. Was she falling in love with the monsieur, the controversial figure in political liberty? Madame Alexandrine's husband? Also, was he falling in love with her? How possible was it?

She continued to eat her lunch, hardly noticing what she ate.

"You don't quite look like you're here."

The words were spoken right next to her, but she barely heard them. Anette knew that she was far away. She smiled and returned to her work. It took long seconds for the dreamer to hear her.

"Did you just say something?" she asked.

Anette, who had turned the other way towards the sideboard, turned back to the girl and smiled again.

"Yes, I did. You heard it now?" she asked, not really expecting an answer.

Jeanne was embarrassed. The smile on Anette's face was evident. She wondered if Anette was reading her mind, and with that thought, she heard even more.

"Are you in love? Your face says it all."

Jeanne was stunned. Had Anette seen her in the hallway, with the monsieur? Did she know that she was in love with him?

"In love? Me? With who?" She slipped out her quivering words.

Anette smiled again at the panic she saw in the young girl.

"You look so troubled. I just asked if you were in love 'cause you were looking far into the rain outside, so dreamy and your face was glowing."

"Does that mean I'm in love?" the young girl asked with a smile.

This time, Jeanne looked calm or at least tried her best to be, but it didn't make any difference to Anette who was too much of an expert in anything of the sort.

"My hair didn't get grey early. I passed your sweet age long ago. There's no way that you can't be," she said.

She turned to Jeanne and leaned on the sideboard, looking straight into the young girl's eyes. Jeanne looked down, trying to hide her smile. She was in love. She definitely was. Her smile was saying it all. Her face was impossible to find; the girl triumphed in her effort to hide her face. At the end of Anette's unsuccessful search, she turned back to her work. Jeanne was happy about it. Now she was sure that Anette hadn't witnessed any beautiful happening between her and her lover. She returned to her lunch and Anette left, having done her work.

"Little lover girl," she softly said with a smile, as she passed Jeanne.

Jeanne was stunned, but she still tried to hide her excitement, although it was futile. There was no way that she could protect her lovely emotions from the mature one. However, she wasn't disturbed by her comments. In fact, she enjoyed them. Anette didn't know whose lover girl the little dressmaker was. How interesting!

Jeanne quickly finished her lunch and returned to the sewing room. She could hardly concentrate on anything. There was a lot of sewing to be done, but she kept dragging her work. She had more to think about. A beautiful moment had passed. It was a little secret, a secret that she had to hide from everyone. She had just become the *little lover girl* of a very dominant figure, and not even for a moment she had any overwhelming thoughts of remorse about falling in love with Alexandrine's husband. It was out of the question. Speaking truthfully, it didn't even cross her mind, so she just let things flow and gave no force on them.

She went back to her sewing, although she was far away from any dressmaking. She feared that she would go wrong, but also had a strong feeling that she wouldn't. Her duties were completed in a sprightly manner. She wondered if the man she longed to see would pay a visit to her. It would have been a beautiful little phenomenon if he had.

She sat at the sewing machine, concentrating on her work. There was a clear view through the window. The rain was gradually coming to an end. It had created some kind of beauty. Yes, the afternoon was decorated by the rain that had just ended. It was neither sunny nor rainy, the best time for a pleasurable walk. But she didn't fancy walking outside now. She thought the trees out there might catch her in love. Birds, coming out after the rain, might sing about her. She paid more attention to the gown she was making. It really matched the wearer. Yes, it did. It was an old-fashioned one, and the wearer wasn't a young beauty.

She looked at herself in the mirror, admiring the young girl bubbling in youth, and fell in love with her own dress, which was more modern than the one she was making. It attracted her eyes much more, and she could remember what a brief time she had taken to do it. Of course, a very long time was taken to do Alexandrine's gown, although it didn't have the same allure.

Suddenly Jeanne's eyes were taken by something unexpected that appeared outside; it was her delight, her longing. There was nothing significant about it from her perspective, except for the cause of it: the dynamic figure, the controversial novelist, Émile Zola. Something had begun to happen when she was eating lunch, although she didn't know.

The monsieur had been disappointed looking at his own appearance, trying to figure out how he could regain his youthful charm; it was impossible. He was never a fan of his large physique; he thought it was unattractive. So, there had to be some way to get the girl. The rain had ended, making it the right time to put his plan into action. He had come out. Soon, he had found his friend outside; it hadn't been used for quite a long time and had almost rusted.

The bicycle was his best friend, and he was happy, going circles. That was just the start. He got used to it in no time and soon headed out of his own yard to reach the road. This was an excellent method of losing weight to be the obsession of a young girl; perhaps he would look charming in her eyes.

The weather was excellent, and his bicycle took him where he wanted to go, at the same speed. He rode for a long time and arrived at the Marsanne. He wasn't sure if Thérèse still lived there, but the Marsanne didn't look like it wasn't occupied. He was very sure that it was inhabited. He looked at the balcony and the adjoining window, trying to measure the distance between them and Julien's little lodge. It was a very short distance. He wondered how appealing the music coming from Julien flute would have been, to attract Thérèse. How flattered he would have been thinking that Thérèse had fallen in love with him! The monsieur felt sorry for Julien, again placing himself in him. They both were, no doubt, in similar situations. He wondered if his alluring seamstress would make use of him in the same manner. But no! It was impossible. She was far from being a Thérèse. She had silently shown him all her love, and there was no trace of doubt in it.

His heart stopped for a moment. He thought he was Julien—the helpless man trying to entice a haughty young woman. For Julien, it was his flute and the music he played. But he, the great novelist who was a prominent figure in political liberty, was much more different, riding a bicycle, overlooking the fact that the girl was in love with him anyway.

He pictured the two strong characters, Thérèse and Julien, in their respective places, both at their windows, one admiring the melody of the other. The former was placed at the sophisticated end and the latter, at the opposite. Oh, how she deliberately hoodwinked him, making him believe that she loved him and later ended up using the very same weapon to be freed of Colombel's dead body! He suddenly began to think of Colombel's role, wondering why it didn't appeal to him much. Well, there was no seemingly apparent reason, at least nothing more than the effect: He wasn't Colombel; he was Julien himself.

He returned to his bicycle and rode it at a very high speed. It was definitely a wonderful experience to ride in the countryside. Memories of Julien, Thérèse, and Colombel, disturbed him, however. He remembered his unexpected meetings with Julien, sometimes in town, vague but unforgettable.

Julien had worked as a clerk in the post office. On his way to work, he had received his midday meal from an old woman in the neighbourhood, and he had been very grateful to her, humbly grabbing his lunch from her every morning.

Once, in the post office, he had met a dominant figure in political liberty, Émile Zola. They had met face to face at the counter, but Julien had made no indication of recognition. He had done his service, letting the man leave with satisfaction. But the great novelist had begun to sympathize with the unattractive man. He had continuously attempted to converse with him during this very significant postal service. The clerk hadn't shown interest in any kind of communication, except the formal one. So, the controversial novelist had left with the faint idea of including him in his own art. He had done it later, although in an unexpected way, as he had never expected such horrible news about Julien in connection with Thérèse and Colombel.

He came back, stopped at the Marsanne again and glanced at Thérèse's balcony, wondering if he was right in his assumption. When the bodies of Colombel and Julien had been drawn from the lake, he had panicked more than anyone else. So, it hadn't been without any reason that Julien had settled into his mind, after their very brief meeting in the post office. How strange!

There had been a lot of rumours about their sudden death, caused by drowning in the lake. Colombel and Julien hadn't been on good terms with each other anyway. Julien had often been teased by young Colombel at their brief meetings in town. It had resulted in mild arguments between them in public. Many people had witnessed these ongoing disturbances between them. So, the most obvious reason for the drowning had been this falling out, in the eyes of the majority. Perhaps they had begun to fight. Perhaps it had happened that evening, in the dark. Perhaps they had accidentally fallen into the lake during their fight. No other speculation had risen.

But the great novelist had, of course, had his own assumptions about it. He had been observing Thérèse very closely. Knowing very well about Thérèse's involvement with Colombel and Julien, there had been nothing else left to consider, except what he had, indeed, been thinking. What contribution had Thérèse had in this tragic fate of the two men?

He had known the truth about the sudden death of the two men, or so he had thought. His imagination had been able to fancy that much. He had envied his imagination and had kept adding more to it. It had been pleasurable, except for the agony felt at the two deaths. Thérèse wasn't the sympathetic kind. She was unconcerned about almost everyone except herself. But how could she have contributed to the loss of the two lives? True, she was cold and unsympathetic, but it didn't mean that she could commit a murder. Also, there hadn't been any reason to do so, or so had been Zola's incredible assumption. One had been Colombel, her secret lover, and the other had been unattractive Julien, who had silently loved her with the miserable belief of being loved by her.

Zola had ended up with plenty to think about. He hadn't been able to give up the unseen involvement in the context, which had been no one else's but Thérèse's. How efficiently could Naturalism play its role in impermanence? What had been the role of impermanence in this context, anyway?

He had begun to visualize the innocent man, Julien, the harmless soul who had sometimes been seen taking walks with his dog. The dog had been his only friend, no different from a human, a huge white dog that had loved its master, understanding him perfectly. Julien had sometimes starved, to give his dog its meal. However, one gloomy day, the saddest incident had taken place. His dog had been poisoned by someone. It had been the biggest loss of his life. His whole world had collapsed, and he had behaved as if dead. He had dug the ground up in an open field and had buried his only friend on his day of mourning, making sure to build a tomb. Every day he had gone to work, passing the dog's grave, giving his lost friend due respect. Really, a part of him had died with the dog. He had been that much of an innocent, harmless man, never capable of committing any kind of evil.

The great writer had kept thinking beyond his most considered thoughts, trying to find some subtle reason why Julien's normal, everyday life would have been that affected. Had he been anything but innocent and harmless, perhaps under exceptional circumstances? What could these exceptional circumstances have been, for that matter? Could Thérèse's pretended love that she had hoodwinked him with, have made some kind of change in Julien that had turned him into a wicked villain who had tried to destroy Colombel? But why would Thérèse have thought of doing any such harm to Colombel? He had been her lover, and she had never thought of destroying him. But could there have been some contradicting situation that would have instigated her to act differently? Well, anything could have been possible. And that was how inconsistent the human mind was. But what could have been the reason? A great artist had enough capacity to fathom reasons. Was it important whether they were factual or not? Well, for the artist, it was immaterial, but it was indeed the kingdom of the individual, so he grieved, mostly for Julien.

He had let his thoughts come and go indefinitely, arriving at a possibility, at the end. If Thérèse was the unsympathetic kind, even though she had deeply loved Colombel, could it have possibly been some accident that had resulted in Colombel's death? Perhaps she had wanted Julien's help to rid herself of the corpse of her lover. Perhaps in his attempt to dispose of the body in the lake, he had fallen in there, too. But how convincing had this phenomenon been? Could harmless, innocent Julien have been capable of the evil act of helping Thérèse escape her crime, letting the world be hoodwinked by her? In brief, could he have helped Thérèse to cover her crime, disclosing to the world that it had been just an accident?

The great novelist had sat in his office giving more weight to his thoughts. The heavier his thoughts had been, the better conclusions he had been able to arrive at.

He had referred to the supreme wisdom of the incomparable, reaching a conclusion at last:

Thérèse had successfully provoked Julien into helping her by showing some pretended love. Julien had been over the moon about it. Just for love, for one night's love, Julien had behaved conflictingly. It hadn't been his fancy. That was how inconsistent and impermanent the human mind was. It was the truth about the entirety of living kind, and there was no doubt about it. The human mind was inconsistent and ephemeral. Nothing was permanent or everlasting.

Zola came back to the present from the recall of his assumptions and started concentrating on his bicycle ride. It was time to ride fast. All the way there, he had been slow. He thought of taking a different route, making his new pastime more interesting. Actually, it wasn't a pastime as such; it was a sound practice he could apply to arrive at the best outcome: looking slim. How practical he was! Wasn't it also absurd? He was trying to win the heart of a girl who had already fallen in love with him. And he, too, knew it well. Nothing was stopping him anyway, on his journey in this beautiful endeavour.

On his way back, he stopped by a significant lake. It was a brilliant rendezvous with the two innocents. The great writer wondered how alarmed Julien would have been to discover Colombel still alive, although he and Thérèse had been under the misconception of him being dead. Bewildered, Colombel would have begun the fight with Julien. He would have been stunned to find himself carried by the man who had often been prey to his teasing. The fight would have lasted for some time until they both had ended up, falling into the lake.

The novelist looked around and stopped his eyes at the huge oak tree that stood by the river. Oh, what a lot would have been revealed, if the tree had been able to speak! His eyes kept roaming around as if to find some clue, although he knew very well that there was absolutely nothing there to give any kind of evidence, that would convince him. But certain things around there wanted to tell him something, and they looked like they would speak to him. The abandoned boat and the massive rock by the lake, in addition to the oak tree, were making a great effort.

He spent some time by the lake, trying to picture the two innocents and how uncaring Thérèse would have been, watching the whole scene from her balcony, playing the falsehood of having nothing to do with the tragedy. What cruelty! No, no one could be as wicked as her, definitely not his adorable dressmaker.

The sudden thought of Jeanne brought a smile to his face. He quickly looked at his bicycle. What an attractive little gadget! It was helping him to win a young girl's heart. Really, it was doing nothing. He had just begun cycling, with no promise of losing weight or beginning to look younger. It was only a pure effort.

He climbed on his bicycle again and started to ride slowly. Gradually, his feet began to work faster, pedalling. He was breaking through the wind which was strongly assaulting him. It was a long ride home. The bicycle entered his premises. He promptly got an excellent idea and rode, avoiding the front entrance. He knew the way to the window of the sewing room, and that was where his lovely enthusiasm was now. He moved slowly towards it and stopped further away from the window to see if the girl was there, at her machine. He was right! She was there!

She swiftly raised her head to find what was disturbing her view, while he carefully focused his eyes on the window. They both stopped there, as there was no reason to look further. They had found each other's eyes.

Well, there he stood, the most awaited man in the world. He was one dominant figure, a well-known controversy. She was happy, delighted to see him. She wanted to walk towards him, but the window was barred. Even if it hadn't been so, it wouldn't have been the best decision. There was a handful of people inside the house who would have been troubled to see them together, Alexandrine who owned him being the main consideration, for that matter.

From his side of it, there was nothing significant or insignificant. He had no sentiments about Alexandrine at this time. It was only the young lass and winning her heart that mattered, although he had already won her, anyway. They stayed there for a very long time without taking their eyes away. She knew she had to return to her sewing, but her eyes were refusing to come back. They were that obsessed. He got off the bicycle and placed it against the tree close by, then returned to her. It was a very clear view. There was the window with bars, the maiden inside and the lover at a distance.

He felt that he was a young prince who had come to meet Rapunzel. There was just a little bit to wait then she was going to send down her long hair so that he could hold onto it, climb it and reach her in no time. But, that was an exaggeration. Deep inside, he felt that he was Julien, watching Thérèse in the balcony, Thérèse who had often teased him, sending him kisses. He felt that he was Julien who had enjoyed them. He almost fell into a trance, but she hardly noticed it. He saw Thérèse sending flying kisses to Julien using both hands and Julien, bewildered, placed his fist against his chest as if to ask whether she was sending them to him. Oh, Julien, wake up now! She was just teasing you, nothing else.

The little dressmaker was confused despite her own delight. She wasn't concerned about his appearance or his age. Not even his family ties really mattered to her. She loved him, and that was about it. The bars of the window would have been crushed with her mighty hands if he had called her, but he never did. He was lost in his own thoughts about her barriers which were never barriers to her. Well, they were barriers as long as they were viewed as barriers.

He gave her a smile, and that was enough for her. It was nothing but an invitation. She abruptly stopped everything about the making of the dress. He watched with expectation as she stood up. The bars were broken in no time. They were shattered to the ground. He still kept watching, the biggest wonder of his life. The young lass escaped through the window and emerged before him. How amazing! They were both in each other's arms, covered by the shade. He didn't need any transformations. She was there even before he called her. True, the darkness gave cover, but they didn't really want it. They didn't bother about anyone or anything around them. It was them, just them, in love.

In the same darkness, however, neither of them knew that some men, perhaps from a secret organization, spying on Zola, had discovered their secret love, yes, the enchanting love story of the controversial figure in political liberty and the charming dressmaker.

21st Century

She entered the elevator which took her to the lonely kingdom of the solitary man. He waited for her, yearned for her and longed for her. But she loved him. She extended her heart to him, which gradually spread all over his loneliness. However, her fear still existed, the fear she couldn't reason out, although she triumphantly concealed from him, the only apparent reason for it.

She saw her face in the mirror when she was being taken to the right level in the elevator. Her face was more appealing than ever, but her neck was bruised. She dreaded the sight of it, and it kept reminding her of the previous night, the terror, she still hadn't told him. Her two hands were resting tightly on her face. It made her look frightened and really, she was. It gave some kind of beauty to the little lovely. The elevator stopped, and she walked out, not even thinking of dropping her hands down. Her hands refused to leave her face, so they held onto it. He stood at the door until she came, and as soon as she reached him the door opened wider; they both walked in, locking the door behind.

He was disturbed to see the frightened girl, and at the same time, he liked the frightened face which was more beautiful. It was another exceptionality about her.

"Are you scared?" he asked.

She shook her head as if to say *no*, although she really was. She was led to the table where they worked. He began his dictation, and she began to write. It was another journey to that beautiful history, more than to the story of Thérèse, Julien, and Colombel. It was all about the romance of a controversial figure and a simple seamstress. And he continued the story of the professor and the girl who wrote.

"Zola had a soft heart towards a girl who worked in his house as a laundress. I have touched on it with Julien, who passes a group of laundresses, and among their mockery, he spots a girl who sympathizes with him and tries to stop the others from teasing him. Their eyes meet for a quick second, and they move on from there."

She got the meaning very well and kept writing, expanding his words. She saw the boy steal a look from the kitchen, but she didn't raise her head to look at him or his master.

"Would you like some tea?" he asked, and before she could respond, he spoke again. "The lady would like tea."

She heard him directing the boy, but being focused on writing, she didn't lift her head to see anything around her. However, she knew that some kind of a conversation was going on between the master and the servant, although neither of them spoke. She could slightly see something pass between them, even though it happened quickly.

The boy lifted his hand and brought the tips of his fingers together, close to his mouth, trying to ask his master, in his own sign language, if his visitor would like to eat something. The master didn't know that the young servant had a softness in his heart for her. So, being an excellent cook, the boy wanted to treat the guest the best way he could. Having seen this pantomime, the visitor raised her head to meet the host sitting in front of her and caught him red-handed. It was exciting. He abruptly ended his sign language then and there.

"He's asking if you'd eat anything," he said.

"No, thank you. I'd prefer to have nothing," her modesty replied.

"She'd only have tea," he said.

He spoke as if he was insisting her on having tea, but really, she didn't want to have anything. The boy returned to the kitchen and began making tea, and his master started the dictation again.

"I feel that Julien is a clear resemblance of Zola himself."

The key sentence was said and some more followed. She took them all down and stopped at the main line. It had never occurred to her that Julien was a resemblance of his creator, but now it was evident that the professor bore a definite resemblance of both Julien and his maker. More was read, and she halted at the most painful part.

"Zola was a man of ego and esteem, who respected all opinions but always trusted and worked with his own. He was a lonely man. He had a relationship with the young laundress simply to overcome his loneliness."

It was a conspicuous repetition. The writer's hand stopped at the evaluation. She quickly lifted her head and looked at his face. How brilliantly he spoke about himself! Yes, in the shade of dictating facts about a long-ago, faraway, historical figure, he didn't realize that he was releasing himself to her. It was stunning, amazing and wonderful. She was really mingling herself with the problem of loneliness of the man who was gathering facts about someone else, not really knowing that he was referring to his own forlorn self.

Soon the young boy came with tea served in a cup, a white cup and a saucer with a gold line. He placed the tray on the table, right in front of his lovely guest, and disappeared back into the kitchen.

"Have your tea!" he said, and she took the teacup in her hand.

"Julien reminds me of a middle-aged man in my hometown who used to play the flute in the evenings for the whole neighbourhood. I associated his behaviour in Julien. And I'm very sure that Zola knew these people individually. He's simply written a story that happened among three people he knew: Julien, Colombel, and Thérèse."

The great professor of performing arts went on with the description, and the delicate writer went on writing her fancy. He often repeated, highlighting his passion. He gazed at her from time to time, but she kept ignoring his eyes and the glow in them. In the depth of writing, she saw a combination of Julien, Monsieur Zola, the middle-aged man who played the flute in his hometown and the professor who brought them all together. She felt that they all were one.

"Sir, I have to go to town to get some groceries," the boy said while passing the mighty dictator and the lovely writer.

She looked at him and his master, who nodded his head at the servant, acknowledging his exit. Really speaking, the master liked the boy going to the grocery store at this time. It gave some time for him to be alone with his writer. The boy left, shutting the door, and his master stood up and locked the door behind.

She kept writing while sipping her tea, still reluctant to raise her head to acknowledge his invitation. He became more of an open-hearted man in the absence of a third party. He held her hand attempting to feel the softness of it and abruptly ended his dictation.

"Now, enough of writing. Tell me about you!"

The words were directed at an unexpected time, although it was the best time for him.

"What about me, sir?" She held the same playful tone as she spoke.

"You're simply out of the ordinary."

"Why?"

"Even today, when you came here, you looked frightened. I don't know why."

"Does that make me special, sir?"

"Well, I won't say that. But there's something different about you."

"I'm just normal."

Just then, they were disturbed by the telephone. He stood up to answer the call, and she thought it was convenient timing. It gave her some time alone, so she left the table. The telephone was placed quite at a distance, and she had no doubt that he couldn't see her from there. She walked towards her main interest. It was fascinating, with shelves full of framed photographs. She went through each one of them, trying to make an identification among his bliss. Amidst the pictures, she came across one that portrayed a couple. She quickly recognized them just as he was ending his phone call, and she turned her head swiftly, to see him standing somewhat further behind, observing her.

"Sir, this is your mother and father," she said.

He nodded his head in such a way as to accept what she said, happy about her understanding. She moved away from the photographs and walked up to the window, which gave her a clear view of the city and its sky. He walked towards her slowly and stopped right next to her. It made her comfortably restricted to the place where she stood. She turned away from the window and stood, leaning on the wall, and he began to admire her face, eyes, lips… He didn't enjoy her reluctance and ended up taking her hands and resting them around his neck. She willingly accepted him, and he kept inviting his fabulous visitor in, one who was waking up his abandoned self. She was in his arms listening to the whispers of her heart.

Monsieur Zola thy lonely self,
I witness after those silent years.

Lost in a world of her own, she hardly realized that she was gradually getting lost within his frame. She was woken up suddenly by his rhythmical words, which echoed melodiously in her ears.

"Can I take you just like this, straight inside?"

She looked into his eyes at the outburst and felt that he was hesitating, as a result of the disapproval which he believed to be present in her.

"No!" she said with a smile and shook her head to communicate how she felt or never felt.

He smiled and let go of his own words while accepting everything that stood on the other end of his loneliness, a beautiful gift from his lovely visitor. He wanted to keep charming her as long as he could, and he tried his best. She tried to speak, but it wasn't possible. However, after a few more efforts, she managed to slip out the words:

"Sir, we're still working. There's a lot to do."

"Why? You don't want to be here with me?"

"Well, it's your work, sir, your work is getting delayed."

He enjoyed her playful tone, and never wanted to let go of her tenderness.

"Yes, it's my work, so let it get delayed."

Her heart stopped for a while, and she felt that she was in a grip that she had no escape from. She wanted to draw herself back, but she could do nothing, as she wished nothing else. He was very intuitive about her and abruptly stopped at the bruise on her neck.

"What's this?"

She remembered the incident of the previous night, and her heart began to dive into the same fear again. However, he didn't have to know anything. At least, for the time being, her identity had to be concealed, so she had to be prompt and give the quickest answer ever.

"Oh, yes, the bruise there, I really don't know how it happened."

She walked towards the table and sat down while he followed, and he soon forgot his question.

"Next Saturday, I'll be in the auditorium for rehearsals," he said with enthusiasm.

She smiled, knowing very well that he was speaking about his main interest.

"Maybe you can visit me there," he said, concluding his first thought.

That was the last thing she expected; she never wanted it. Her gullible self was naturally revealed in a glance. She feared such a rendezvous, just like she feared almost everything around her.

"No, sir," she said. "I can't come there. I'm not directly involved in it. I'm only writing for you."

He stopped at her words and was unable to speak further as the young boy returned home and his writer was almost done with her work. The boy passed them and entered the kitchen, giving the master enough time to speak to his great interest.

"Did you think I'd gulp you down? Is that why you don't want to come?" he asked in a very jovial tone.

"No, how can you gulp me down?" she said in the same playful tone he envied.

"I can do even that if I wanted to," he uttered.

"Oh, now I know."

"What?"

"That you swallow people."

"Yes."

"You're an *anaconda.*"

That made him laugh. He loved her sense of humour. He held her hand, making sure that they weren't in the view of the young servant. His dominant self was affected by the thought that his affection for the young girl would be noticed by his servant. It was ridiculous and not the behaviour expected from his typical nature. But that was what he was, and there was nothing more to it. He ended up kissing her hand and releasing it as quickly as possible. She was stunned as it was strikingly unexpected but had to ask him a question. It wasn't easy, but after several attempts, she slipped the words out.

"Sir, you told me that other girls also help you with this." She paused before she found the right words.

"Yes..." he said, waiting for the rest of her query.

"Do they come here often?"

"Yes."

"How often?"

"Just to complete their work, yes, they come."

He smiled to himself, reading her mind.

"Not only that," he said.

"Then what?" She became curious. He looked at the kitchen again, trying to see if the boy was in his vicinity, and was satisfied when he wasn't.

"I hold them in my arms, even closer than this."

She became silent at his words. She thought they were firm, although she knew that he was merely enjoying her query. However, his words made her silent. She turned back to her work and started writing. It was a futile attempt. Her pen was doing the job tentatively, but she was trying. She looked at his face and realized that he was far away. She was right. He mingled with the historical figure once again.

"The Dreyfus Affair was one with significance. He fought for his friend, who was wrongly accused of treachery. His open letter to the president had a great influence on the release of his friend. He went out of his way to clear his name."

She went on writing his heart, although none of it really interested her. The dictation went on, with him admiring her clear, sharp face. They both looked at each other at the same time. She was overwhelmed by the sorrow in his eyes. He was very calm, and she decided that it was the best time to convey her discovery, for the second time, that *Pour Une Nuit D'Amour* was different from what it turned out to be.

"Sir, I have something to tell you."

"What? Is it the same thing that you often try to say but end up not saying?"

His question entirely changed her mood, as it reminded her of her present agony and her identity. She wanted to communicate the right information about his first direction, but the professor misunderstood her. Anyway, it was the best time to reveal the facts.

"No, sir. This…"

"Oh, keep it to yourself! I don't know about it, and I don't even want to know about it. I'm just tired of listening to those same words, '*I have something important to say*,' but you never say it."

He silenced her again with all his might, and she wasn't able to convey the real story to him, revealed to her from history itself. There was no way that she could communicate the truth. She still had the idea of conveying it through the boy, but it was becoming a fantasy now.

And so, he began Zola's story, which was really, his self-description.

"It was only when he died that his name was cleared of many accusations," he said.

She was astonished to hear him say this and to hear the meaning behind his words. He was again going parallel with history. He had his hand on hers as if he was asking something. She was sympathetic, promising him the best. She listened most earnestly to the set of words that followed. But the words rested within himself, without really being spoken. He managed to use the relevant words only, referring to history although he was really telling his own story.

"What's the use of his name being cleared when he was dead?"

She listened to his story of woe with a broken heart, trying to figure out how she could address it.

"Do you know, at one point in his life, he was so broke that he even ate the sparrows that came on his windowsill?"

The young writer felt broken. Far behind his face, through the window, she saw gulls flying towards the sea. She wondered whether they would come to his windowsill just to make friends with him. But she was sure that he wouldn't make them his meal unless he was dangerously engrossed and lost in his loneliness.

Soon after the dictation, she bade him farewell and started towards home. It was time for another beautiful sequence of investigation. She entered her little home, her comforting place. What a day! Past and present mingled together! She had a lot on her hands now. No sooner had she thought this than she found herself travelling through the work again. It was a much more wonderful journey this time. She met them again, the pretty dressmaker and the controversial French novelist. He was there seated in his library and she, in the sewing room. The young writer found her quite easily, appropriately doing her dressmaking. She sat right in front of the seamstress, the pure heart, the young charm. There was no disturbance in any way. So, she made her way to the library. And, there she found him, the greatest historical novelist: Émile Zola.

She looked into his eyes and found nothing but grief in them. There was more to the story of this man of esteem. What she could see now was sheer loneliness, sorrow, and distress. She saw the host of birds that danced outside. Confused, she walked towards the window, unsure of their breed. The birds looked at the girl who was watching them as if to ask them their identity. She smiled at them, and they sang to her. She was right. They were sparrows.

She turned back to the man of excellence who was still seated with his eyes aimed far away through the window. She stood in front of him and started examining his face which was a story.

Controversial French novelist,
Major figure in political liberty,
Proponent of Naturalism,
I ink my pen to write thyself.

Monsieur Zola, thy lonely self,
I witness after those silent years.
So broke relied on sparrows on a sill,
Thy lonely self vigorously shines.

She ended up humming the beautiful verse, her own creation. It didn't belong to the seamstress; it came straight from the writer. However, something remarkable happened right after the lovely piece of recitation, something the young writer hadn't expected. His majestic self gave a slight smile at the gift and rose to his feet as if he suddenly remembered something. She moved aside to make way for him. He was quick and walked like a shooting arrow; she rushed behind him.

It was the best examination ever, and she never gave up. He took the most extended way and finally reached the sewing room. His quick walk made little noise, so Jeanne didn't know that he stood there at the door. The writer was much more intuitive than the dressmaker. She knew that the lover had arrived.

Jeanne was still doing her needlework, her mind entirely focused on it. She didn't realize that he had come until he stood right behind her, and in the blink of an eye, they were in each other's arms.

19th–20th Century

They were making love, giving no consideration to the danger that it might bring. It was a brawl of making love. No one in the household knew about their stunning intimacy. Alexandrine wasn't considered by either of them. She didn't exist. Jeanne fell on the sewing machine; enticing her was much easier than Zola had assumed. She could hardly be seen. They were embracing each other very passionately that they even forgot to breathe. It was passion at its highest. To a third person viewing them, they looked like just one, not two.

However, they both paused as Zola was drawn back by a noise he heard outside, although Jeanne heard nothing. She was too far inside him to hear anything, except his breath and heartbeat, so she was disappointed by his sudden withdrawal, and waited for his quick return. He realized that he had stepped back for an unimportant little sound, so he returned immediately, reimbursing the few seconds missed.

She wanted to whisper some words, but it was impossible now. She was a delicate one, strengthened by him. Throughout, she had her arms around him, and that was what he wanted. He whispered some words, very briefly.

"I was waiting, waiting and waiting for you."

With much effort, Jeanne spoke in a murmur.

"What will happen if madame finds out? If Anette comes here now and sees us?"

He smiled at the girl's worry.

"Anette is busy in the kitchen, and Alexie's out now, though you don't know."

"You mean she's gone out?"

"Yes, she wasn't even in when you came this morning, and she'll be back by evening."

"Oh, that's why."

"What do you mean, *that's why*?"

"That's why you're here, monsieur?"

"I'd have come to you anyway," he said embracing her lightly this time.

He rested his head on her curved lap, and she sat down feeling his forehead with her fingers. It was the most comfortable place for him, but he thought that they were both quite uncomfortable in the sewing room. They needed a better place, a room consisting of a bed. But, right now they didn't have it.

They stayed there just like that for quite a long time, then he gradually got ready to leave. Jeanne was left in the sewing room in contemplation. She was never going to end her passionate tale with her lover, the monsieur, but some alternative had to be implemented to meet him. Sewing room wasn't the best place. She sat there in her sewing seat, not knowing how long she had her mind at work. Finally, she arrived at a brilliant conclusion and decided to make it happen soon.

Alexandrine returned home, and that was when Jeanne realized that it was already evening and almost time for her to leave. She was worried when she saw the clock. It was very late, and she couldn't complete any of the work, planned for the day. Also, she knew that she could do nothing else with the rest of the day. She folded the dress materials and covered the sewing machine. The window had to be closed tightly before she left, the window with the broken bars; she had dashed them down to reach the monsieur. She panicked for a moment, wondering how they could be fixed again. That was a momentary thought before she had her body weight on the sewing machine to lock it. It was a stunning view: Jeanne leaning on the sewing machine. There was a difference between now and earlier when she had fallen on it. It was more beautiful now, in a way.

She looked at her reflection in the mirror. Her face was glowing, and she looked more beautiful than when she arrived at work that morning. She fell on her back, on the same sewing machine, trying to figure out how she would have looked earlier with the monsieur, the most dominant man in the world, and she could see nothing but her fragility and tenderness. She was a delicate little rose that had just blossomed.

She rose swiftly as she heard someone enter the sewing room and saw that it was Anette. However, she couldn't stand up before she was seen.

Anette caught the young girl in action, and she walked towards her with a brilliant smile.

"Are you trying to fall asleep there?" she mockingly asked.

Jeanne was frightened, thinking of the worst. Specifically, her best bet was that Anette had witnessed her earlier, in the same spot, with the monsieur. But, truthfully, no one in the house knew about their *unmatched love*; there was no other suitable label for it. However, Jeanne stood there speechless as she had no excuse for her unusual position on the sewing machine. Anette understood the young girl's change, which had really begun to show quite recently. Her obvious guess was right. Jeanne was in love. Yes, she definitely had a lover, and she was experiencing the healing power of love for the first time in her life. Her present dreaminess was an excellent bit of evidence towards it.

Anette didn't want her young friend to worry about any of the comments she made, so she quickly changed the topic before Jeanne fell into a higher level of embarrassment.

"Are you not going home today? It's quite late."

"I was just closing. That's when you came."

"Madame wants to talk to you before you leave today."

Jeanne was alarmed when she heard the last few words; they entered her ears like a flash of fire. Perhaps Alexandrine sensed something that she never should have, and that was why she wanted to see her. Yes, most obviously the superior wished to question the seamstress about the relationship, the lovely connection or the beautiful affair she was having with her husband. It was clear that Jeanne had no escape now. She had nothing left to do, except to answer her. She looked at Anette and reconfirmed with herself that Anette had no idea about it.

No sooner was Anette gone than Jeanne went up to the mirror to examine her appearance. She took a closer look at her face and also her neck. The deep cut in her blouse exposed more of her neck and the area around it; she was stunned by a very obvious redness. She tried to cover it with her collar but failed. It could never be hidden, as it wasn't close to her clothing. Alexandrine was going to notice it; Jeanne had no doubt about it.

She closed the room, took her belongings and walked all the way to the living room where she met Alexandrine sitting next to the fire. It was the same armchair, the same position, and the same gaze. Her legs began to tremble when she saw her, although there was absolutely no change in Alexandrine whose behaviour was the same.

Jeanne was stopped by her own fear at the sight of her superior. She thought she was going to receive the biggest admonition in the world. The two had their eyes on each other, although they were at a distance, one standing and the other sitting. But they could hardly look into each other's eyes.

"Why are you standing there, my dear? Come close to me!" Alexandrine said.

Jeanne was more frightened to hear her voice, and her words made her move forward in utter fright that the beauty of her elegant neck and the area around would be seen. With lots of effort, she put up a smile and stepped forward.

"Sit down!"

The next command was given in a very gentle manner, and Jeanne thought that Alexandrine was trying her best to be kind to her. Was she hiding her rage with some pretended compassion? Jeanne didn't stop to find any answers to her questions, but she made herself fall on the chair in front of her superior. And so, began Alexandrine:

"How do you find the work? Are you enjoying it or is it a little too much?"

The dressmaker was posed a question that she hadn't expected; she had imagined a muddle in the highest extreme. She ended up giving a modest reply. "I'm managing well, madame."

"Now, I called you here to ask something very important…," Alexandrine paused for a few seconds before she came up with the necessary words, making Jeanne panic even more.

"There's a lot more sewing coming up, and you'd have less time to finish them all. Will it be possible for you to live in until the work is complete?"

Alexandrine made her request, and it was a huge surprise for Jeanne, who was flabbergasted now. This was the last she had expected, and she was happy and sad about it. She looked straight into Alexandrine's face and saw that she was looking through her. She became suspicious of her superior's startling request but was reassured of the nonexistence of any other reason, except what was being conveyed to her. Alexandrine really did want her to work as a live-in dressmaker, and she had no distrust on her at all. So,

Jeanne was convinced that she was in a bogus fear of Alexandrine knowing the beautiful secret.

Jeanne's silence was most disliked by Alexandrine, but she still gave her time to mention her decision. However, it was taking longer than she had expected, so she enhanced the offer.

"Don't you like my suggestion? I'll increase your pay, and you'll have a separate room in the house for yourself."

Jeanne felt terrible for making Alexandrine repeat the question. It was just a question for her and not a demand or a request, so she thought there was no reason to refuse. Of course, there was one pretty reason to accept it, a reason hidden from Alexandrine and the rest of the world. And she ended up answering affirmatively, indeed.

"Yes, madame, I will do it. I surely can work, living in."

Alexandrine was startled by the response. At first, the girl was silent, without a word for a long time, and then there was a very positive, rather dramatic outburst. She was calm and collected, listening to the rest of her response.

"I know there's a lot more to do. I'm fighting with time to do all of it. It's a good idea! It's a great idea!"

Despite all the confusion about Jeanne's sudden change, Alexandrine was very happy that she accepted the offer. She enjoyed the jubilant reaction of the girl.

"So, when can you start?" she asked.

"I can even start tomorrow," Jeanne replied.

"Oh, that's wonderful. So, you can leave now and come ready tomorrow. I won't keep you long."

Soon, Jeanne left with her heart full, for the next day. She wondered if the master of the house even knew about the change in her work schedule. She wondered if it was his decision put into words by Alexandrine. Whatever it was, she was happy that her lovely neck wasn't a concern. It was only she who knew how beautiful it was and no one else, just no one else. Excellent!

Next morning, none of them really knew that the wondrous writer from the future was visiting them. However, this time her findings differed, and things were taking an unexpected turn. She wandered in the monsieur's house, unable to find either of them. She walked to the library to find it empty. Through the window, she saw a host of sparrows, but the monsieur wasn't there to welcome them, listen to them or rely on them for anything. She walked into the sewing room, and Jeanne wasn't there. There was no trace of her. She was disheartened. Next, she approached the kitchen. All she had to do was, go in, but she was reluctant. Instead, she walked to the bedroom arranged for Jeanne. It was a neat little room, well organized. She was just about to leave when suddenly something took her by its will. She walked towards it, knowing that something was hiding behind the curtain, and she drew it open to find the dark sky with its shiny twinkles.

It was she, the girl who wrote, who was in the room now, not the one who seamed, and she felt that the stars were taking her somewhere, to some faraway city where a lovely pair was voyaging through history. How enchanting! Where was she now? Future, present, past or somewhere in between? She wasn't sure, nor did she want to know. She was just amazed, charmed and obsessed.

She wondered what Jeanne would have been doing by night. Well, she would have been longing for the monsieur. What would she have been doing until they first met? Looking through the window at the night sky, thinking about her triviality compared with the galaxy, just like the future writer did? She doubted it.

She kept watching the stars, wondering if they were the same ones she saw from her balcony, not knowing how different they were from those in the present. Well, what could remain unchanged? Just nothing, nothing at all. Everything was subject to change, and so were the stars. The same stars she saw from her balcony had gone through severe changes over the century, although she could hardly perceive them. The human mind went through much more drastic changes, just like Zola described in his realistic, fictional character: Julien. If innocent Julien, far from being innocent, had helped Thérèse dispose of Colombel's dead body, for the promise of one night's love, what couldn't change in the human mind? The answer was left in the inconsistent, ephemeral human mind and nowhere else.

She quietly withdrew herself and walked into the kitchen, where she found Anette with the other kitchen staff. Disappointed, she quickly came out and made her way to the living room, where she found Jeanne at last. She was in a deep conversation with Alexandrine.

Alexandrine rested herself well, sitting on the couch listening to what the seamstress had to say. Having their eyes directed at each other, they spoke quietly, only as loud as they needed. It wasn't clear if Alexandrine knew about the lovely love story that went on in her own house. But she was very kind to Jeanne, and so was Jeanne to her. The young dressmaker had no ill will nor did she ever think about how badly Alexandrine would have been affected if she had ever found out. In brief, she was too young to realize the severity of it. How could she, when the monsieur himself never considered it?

Jeanne's voice lulled, and Alexandrine was pleased, heartbreakingly amazed. She listened to her with her whole self. But Jeanne had arrived with the unexpected.

"Madame, I have something to tell you."

Alexandrine had least expected her at this time. Jeanne was looking disturbed, although she tried her best to pretend the contrary. Her dress was crushed like paper, her hair tousled, and her face troubled. Alexandrine was worried. In fact, she hadn't seen Jeanne in this plight before, for now, she was a clear contrast to the sparkling youth she always had been.

"What's wrong, Jeanne? You're not looking so good this morning. You were very happy when you left yesterday."

Jeanne's mind ran to the previous night. She had gone home, very happy, with the intention of starting at a new schedule, to be a live-in seamstress. But she had been halted by the same men who had once watched them at night. First, they had followed her in the dark, before catching up with her. The topic had been, of course, Zola, the gigantic figure in political liberty, the interest of many sources. They had looked like they might try to overpower her and force her to do something, but she wasn't sure of anything. They had walked very close, right next to her, as if to take her in a capture, encircling her while walking. She was sure that they knew about her and her present involvement with the monsieur, but she didn't know how. They had spoken very loudly, asking her when she might meet him next. The whole incident had frightened her, ending up in her own sudden decision. It wasn't advisable to visit the monsieur's house daily or work there, living in. The strangers had implied that they were going to get some underhand work done by her. She had to do everything to shield him, and he had to be informed.

"Madame, I'm sorry to say. I don't think I can work here any longer."

Alexandrine was alarmed to hear her. That was the last thing she had expected to hear. The young seamstress had been very helpful with the sewing in the house. She was an excellent dressmaker, brilliant with any type of needlework. The needle was her favourite tool, and she did wonders with it. Today she was expected to start as a live-in.

"Sorry, I didn't hear you well," Alexandrine said.

She was making her best attempt to act like she was in a daze and had not heard her well, knowing very well that she understood what was said to her. Jeanne hesitated to repeat herself as she was more affected than Alexandrine. There was plenty that Alexandrine was in the dark about and Jeanne knew it. That was precisely what kept her silent about the current facts, not her fluency in maintaining silence on common knowledge. Knowing the truth well, Jeanne almost came down to a level of overreaction and tried to seek confession, but she controlled herself before it was too late.

"Madame, I can't work here any longer."

This time, Alexandrine couldn't avoid her words or her own senses, knowing that her intelligence worked very well. But she wasn't happy to hear what Jeanne was informing her of.

"May I ask why?"

Jeanne was speechless at her question. She had no valid reason to give, except the real one, which she was never revealing.

"Madame, I just miss home. I can't live here. I want to live with my own family."

"Aren't we your family, Jeanne?"

Alexandrine asked an appropriate question, not knowing that it was so. It was only Jeanne who knew that she had begun her little family there, but she maintained the same silence, giving just a vague smile. Alexandrine spoke again.

"Perhaps, you simply need a break. Perhaps when you spend some time with your family, you might want to come back again."

"I just want to stay home," Jeanne repeated.

It wasn't clear who was losing, Alexandrine, Jeanne or both. Well, if Alexandrine was in the dark, then Jeanne was living in extreme darkness.

"For a brief period? And you return later?"

It seemed like Jeanne couldn't escape Alexandrine's request that easily. She was silent for a very brief time until she realized that she had to quickly make the best of the question she was asked and offer an answer.

"Yes madame, I just need a break, perhaps for a brief time, but for now, I need to be home."

"So, you will come back?"

Jeanne couldn't avoid her question, and she couldn't positively answer it, either. So, she smiled again, a very faint smile.

"How have you done with the work?" Alexandrine asked.

"I've done well, madame. I've completed everything for now," Jeanne confirmed.

"Well, you can leave now. I'll come to the sewing room in a while."

Jeanne walked towards the sewing room, hoping that she would meet the monsieur on her way. But she didn't. The best place to meet him was at the library, so she changed her route and started towards it, making sure that no one saw her. And yes, he was there. He was at the table, working, his eyes aimed through the window. Before he saw her, she looked through the window to see a knot of sparrows in a sprattle, and he didn't look like he was taking his eyes away from them. He seemed disturbed for some reason that she didn't know. Anyway, he had to be told about the men she had encountered. She stepped towards him, and he briskly took his eyes away from the birds to find the girl in front of him. He didn't look like he was happy to see her.

"Monsieur, yesterday…," Jeanne said, beginning to relate.

"So, what about yesterday?"

"Yesterday night…"

"Now, don't tell me anything!"

"Monsieur, this is important. I came to tell you that yesterday…"

"Please leave! Don't disturb me!"

Jeanne made many unsuccessful attempts to have him informed. Perhaps he didn't know that he was being spied on by some men. Anyway, she wasn't successful in revealing it to him. He spoke as if he was irritated. Anyway, spending time in the library wasn't the best choice, so she withdrew herself.

She walked away and entered the sewing room as quickly as she could. Alexandrine would come soon, so she had to have the room more organized than it was. She began to tidy up the room, hurrying her hands, taking less time to give the best impression. She was done very soon, and she rested herself at the window, looking outside.

Outside was the same, where the monsieur had once come on his bicycle just to catch a glimpse of her. She watched, holding the bars of the window, to see if he would come again, although his arrival was impossible now. But he did, yes, in a kind of eclipse. He stopped in the shade of the same tree, watching her, and she wondered if she was going to find her relief, escaping through the bars again. Suddenly, the danger she had encountered on her way home, the night before, was beginning to fade away. The monsieur hadn't listened to her anyway, and she decided to leave him undisturbed about it.

The sky was bright. No doubt, the same planets existed, but she couldn't see them during the day, and she was happy. No stars were apparent to emphasize her insignificance. Only the monsieur was standing out there, and she stretched out her hands. He called her. She was just about to emerge when she felt a hold on her shoulder. It was Alexandrine!

She was shaken by the sudden touch, and she loathed it; she loathed anyone disturbing her beautiful dream, her illusion.

"You look like you're in a happy mood. Well, happy to go back home?" Alexandrine asked.

Again, it was another question in need of an answer and Jeanne was quick.

"Yes."

"Now, you look much better than when you spoke to me this morning. Keep smiling! Your smile is rewarding. Anyway, I'm sad to let you go. I was expecting you to live in. But I'm sure you'll come back soon. I still don't understand why you changed your mind, all of a sudden."

Jeanne smiled again, and Alexandrine turned to examine the room. All fabrics were folded on the shelves, and she was satisfied. She saw the ironed clothes, ready to be delivered. There was nothing ready to be stitched, as the young dressmaker was done with everything, and it made her doubtful for a quick second.

"Looks like you've completed almost everything. There's absolutcly nothing more to do."

"Oui, madame."

"So, you were planning to leave us, even though you were hoping to start living in?"

At this question Jeanne became silent again, finding the right words to answer her. It was a *yes* or *no* answer. Alexandrine was right in her doubt to a very great extent.

"Were you, Jeanne?" she asked again, turning away from her.

Going on with her inspection, nothing more spoken, she wasn't really looking for an answer to her question. She was happy, definitely happy with the work brilliantly done by the dressmaker she was going to lose, not knowing that she had lost her long before.

"It's excellent, Jeanne," she said, full of appreciation.

"Merci, madame," Jeanne replied with a brilliant smile.

Alexandrine was more stunned to see the change in Jeanne, transitioned from the distressed girl to a happy one again. It was surprising for her. She little knew that the monsieur had appeared in the window, but only for the pretty dressmaker, in her untouched dream.

"You look happy, Jeanne, all of a sudden. What made you change so quickly? In the morning, you were very worried."

Jeanne couldn't express herself in words, as they would have been the biggest thunderstroke on Alexandrine. Well, the monsieur had appeared in the window, confirming to her that he was still living in her heart, even if they weren't in touch. No matter how disturbed he was, she knew that he would come looking for her.

"You're very happy to go back home, aren't you Jeanne?" Alexandrine asked.

"Yes," Jeanne replied, with her heart full.

She walked back to the window to see if he was still there, but he wasn't. She knew that she wasn't returning home alone. He would visit her one day, and she was going to wait until then.

She turned back to the room to find that Alexandrine was gone, so she was happy to be left alone. She was going back home for the monsieur, very confident that he would follow her, although such liveliness existed in her heart and nowhere else. Most certainly, she couldn't bear his absence. Well, no one knew that she was his *second wife*, really, the *other wife*.

The monsieur was busy in the library. A few sparrows flew towards his window and perched on the sill, reminding him of his miserable past.

Sparrows were remarkable birds that he had relied on, some time ago, but that was when he found them on his windowsill with no life in them. What a terrible past!

He had ample time, and he was going to make use of every single moment. He counted every second that passed until sunset, but of course, there was much to do before darkness fell, most definitely the bicycle rides. The beautiful rides were more ridiculous now, for they were done to lose weight and become slim, to attract and win the heart of a pretty maid he had amazingly won. It didn't stop him, anyway. By afternoon, he was out.

Whether he was losing weight or not was out of the question, but he ended up riding to the Marsanne wondering if he could catch a glimpse of Thérèse. Marsanne was a grand building. He rode around it and stopped where he believed the little lodge where Julien lived, was. Ruins of it were still there, and he stood among them, having a clear view of Thérèse's balcony and the window.

It was twilight, and of course, darkness was gradually emerging—the best time of the day. In a while, a female figure appeared at the window facing the balcony, and the monsieur was devastated by the very sight of her. It seemed like the figure at the window hardly saw the man on the bicycle down below, who waited for her arrival. The baffled soul stood up from his two wheels and stayed still, without even a slight movement, astonished to the highest degree. True, he had wished to see Thérèse, but he had never assumed that his expectation would come to reality.

He stared at the figure for some time and quickly realized that she would walk onto the balcony soon. He had to do something to hide before it was too late and now was the time. He took charge of the circumstances and quickly took cover behind a huge tree. It was an orange tree, a bushy one, so he and his two wheels took the same cover behind it; it promised him the fullest cooperation. So, it happened just the way he thought it would, and the magnificent moment was on its way.

The pretty woman was bored standing at the window. She walked onto the balcony and stopped leaning on the barrier, resting her hands on her face. There was wonderful mutual support between her hands and face. Her hair fell down reaching her waist, and her face could hardly be seen in the sundown, but the great novelist managed to capture the beauty and malice in it, with heartfelt sympathy for Julien and Colombel.

She kept gazing at the sky, dull and boring, wondering when she would be able to view at least a single star in it. Darkness was gradually falling on her face, and Monsieur Zola was unsuccessfully attempting to have a clear view of her. Some obvious facts were clear to him, even when the maximum level of darkness was finally in effect. Thérèse brought her hands to her red lips. She kissed her fingertips, sending her kisses flying high up in the sky, and the monsieur wondered if she was merely teasing the sky. At the same time, he was having visions of a sympathetic girl from a century in the future. She, too, was standing there on her balcony looking at the sky, but her sky was lit with tiny sparkles. The two girls were incompatible, a sheer mismatch.

Thérèse still had her eyes on the sky, with a certain amount of focus on the little disturbance that came from the orange tree. She knew that something moved behind it but gave less concentration to it, as she never doubted, even for a moment, that there was a lively being there.

Meanwhile, there was a seamstress in her own home. She was relaxing at her window, watching the same dull, uninteresting sky, apparent to Thérèse. There was a vast difference between that pair of girls, too, even if they were admiring the same sky. Having her tender eyes on the road far away, Jeanne was waiting for the monsieur, gazing at the sky from time to time.

Thérèse kept scrutinizing the sky blindly, hoping to find a star in the monotony above, but there wasn't even a slight trace of one. It so happened in the best interest of the sky, anyway. The sky was fortunate not to have any of her children out in the vicinity of a highly dominant woman, who would put those sparkles to her best use or tease them and mock them or use them to conceal her own folly, which she believed was her flair. The great writer stood still behind the tree, admiring the beautiful malice. But his mind turned to return to his pretty lass.

Jeanne, with her grieving eyes still on the road, stood at her window, gripped by the monotonous sky which gave no hope of the monsieur. How pathetic! She forgot about all other existence. He was her lover and no one else's, so she was waiting for him with millions of flowers blooming in her heart. It was taking longer than she expected, so she began to make a braid with her hair, her delicate fingers deftly at work. She, as well as the monsieur, could see the young tenderness from a century in the future, the girl who wrote, taking down vital dictation.

The young writer from the future leaned on the railing of her balcony, watching the beauty of the night sky. It was flowery with its spread of silvery shines, and they looked like they were in a mutual gaze with her. She wondered what they really were. Were they planets where life existed? Were they galaxies, even if they appeared like single stars? Whatever they were, they brought out the beauty of the night sky. Unable to take her eyes away, she stopped at a remarkable little twinkle somewhat separate from the rest. It was startling, and she thought that it was no different from the others. All sparkles looked tiny to her vacant eyes, but they were enormous planets, more than she could imagine. She came back to herself in an instant, wondering how trivial she was. Yes, how insignificant she was, like a wasp, a moth or a firefly!

At the recall of the tiny lives, she turned her head to the light bulb, to find them struggling around it.

21st Century

Her heart began to weep again, so her thoughts were quickly put into action. She ran to the switch button to turn off the light, and her fingers found it quickly. Turning to the bulb, she realized that a heap of insects had fallen down on the ground, just as it happened almost every night. She walked towards the little lives that were struggling. Sitting on the ground, she took a tiny insect to her finger, trying to identify its features and how closer to life it was, than to death, disregarding the impossibility of coming to any assumption about it. The insect, being confident that it was walking on a human, moved all the way along her hand knowing that it was impossible to fly now, and the delicate hand gave all the support it could. The insect escaped to the railing of the balcony, and the hand rushed inside with no proper farewell to the faraway sparkles.

She walked to the kitchen with some heartbreaking words in her lovely dictation, echoing in her.

"It was only after this man died that his name was cleared of many accusations."

How pathetic! The monsieur had faced that pitiful state a century ago. He had died a tragic death, leaving the rest of the world in distress and suspense. His innocence had been discovered but hadn't been able to set him free of the allegations. The professor had very well described this distressful plight, highlighting the parallelism between two centuries.

Her body felt icy cold, so she pulled a blanket from her closet and wrapped it up around her, almost hiding in it. She grieved for his sad plight of being unjustly accused, trying to understand the best way she could, the monsieur and the professor.

Meanwhile, the professor was diving into his own thoughts about his remorseful past. He was fighting with his own memories which mingled with incidents, events, and situations. His favourite resting place was the rooftop of the building, and he often went there to relax in isolation. He loved it but didn't love it.

His mind was running through a newspaper article, recently published. The article was bubbling in his eyes when he read it, and there was no way that he could escape its content. It wasn't very clear if he was repenting over it, but he was affected; it came at a time when his mind was healing from all the miseries. He read through it and behaved as if he was indifferent to it, but his heart was weeping. How much had he lost, in his attempt to acquire what would never be his? He went to a brief nap, with the newspaper resting on his chest. His hands slowly moved down the page while his inward eye was wandering around his house among the photographs.

He stopped at the portrait of a delicate girl who had created an unforgettable drawing. He wept over her as much as she had wept over him. Her hazel eyes were still sparkling in youth, and they took him to decades past.

It had been flowery, very flowery outside and they had held hands, talking about love. Sometimes crystals had rained, soaking them in water, but living in the other one's eyes, they had never even felt it. Things had happened in a flash, much faster than any kind of realization, he being distracted by some greenery. He had abandoned her in the heavy rain and had walked towards the better side of the garden, leaving the pretty tenderness in deep distress to face the loss by herself. Oh, what a tragedy! Being deceived by his own fate, he had never been able to realize it. There hadn't been greenery anywhere. His eyes had been misled by something: an illusion. He had been trapped with no escape. He had turned around quickly to find the biggest surprise, a negative one.

The girl had disappeared, leaving him a loner and he never saw the pretty hazel eyes again.

He suddenly woke up from his daze and realized that the newspaper was still on him, with the right page turned to his face. His eyes took everything in. He stood up from his chair with the same worry and started walking down to his dwelling, and at his approach, the boy opened the door. He walked straight into his room and the boy, who knew every movement of his master, began to worry, understanding his confusion better than anyone else. He observed his master and made sure that he was well cared for, at all times.

He saw him resting in bed, watching the ceiling. Yes, the ceiling was a screen, and his mind was travelling towards the middle-aged man in his hometown playing the flute. He started with the musician and passed by many other significances, the beautiful hazel eyes and many more, stopping at one misfortune that came back to him; it was an arrest. Yes, he could still remember. It had happened at an unexpected time. He had heard the doorbell and hadn't even bothered to come to the front. After exchanging some words, the boy had come inside to inform him of the police visit, knowing nothing about an arrest.

"Police are here to meet you, sir."

The words had entered his ears like a hot coal, perhaps with reasons to fear the police, his own guilt-ridden conscience more than anything else. He had walked to the front, trying his best to hide his heart.

"You're under arrest, sir," one police officer had said, speaking very kindly to him.

He had stopped in front of them saying nothing, and another officer had shown the arrest warrant from the judge, confirming the facts. No sooner than that, handcuffed, he had been taken out, to the police vehicle. He had wanted to call his lawyer but had decided it unnecessary. He still remembered how people had gathered to see him being loaded into the vehicle by the police. He had just looked down, unable to face them.

In the police headquarters, crime investigation department, three officers had sat with him in the inquiry.

"Would you like to have something to drink?" one police officer had asked.

The accused had politely refused the offer. "No, I think we should get down to why I am here straight away."

So, the police had begun their work, a questioning of three hours. They had received instructions from high authorities for the arrest and the inquiry, and the reason had been fair enough.

A murder of a journalist had caused all the unrest in the town. The young journalist had been going home after work, in a trishaw, when a gunman had been aiming at the prey, following the contract he had received earlier. The open trishaw had taken a turn, and the difference on the fatal day had been the emptiness of the road, lessening any additional trouble the killer would have had to take. The trishaw had moved quickly, speeding through the wind, enjoying the beauty of the rustic atmosphere, and so had the passenger, not knowing about the few minutes left for him. The gunman had been hiding in the densely grown grassland, taking careful aim as he had already seen his target speeding along the road. In a few seconds, he had pulled the trigger, and the bullet had flown into his target's head, not even giving him a moment to settle down with it. The driver, in a panic, had rushed the heavily wounded passenger to the hospital, not knowing that he had already taken his last breath.

The professor still had his eyes aimed at the ceiling, feeling remorseful about his miserable past and its consequences. He returned to the policemen and their questioning, again recalling how he had sat there dumbfounded at the accusation. The policemen had been firm, complying with their job description most formally. And the accused had been repeating the same words:

"I have nothing to do with his murder. Besides, why should I be a suspect here? I've done nothing."

"But this journalist was writing against corruption, and he was attacking your party very often in his articles."

"Does that one fact have sufficient proof to say that I was involved in this crime?"

"I'm questioning here, not you. We've had tips from many sources that it was planned by you. His wife informed us that he used to often receive threats from people, and you were one of them."

"Well, she can say that."

"She also informed us that you recently tried to bribe her with money to keep her mouth shut when she was speaking to the media about you."

"She can say that, too."

Very brief answers had been offered in the investigation, which had ended in a few hours with no proper conclusion. He had been set free by the police, as there hadn't been enough evidence to prove him guilty of the crime. He had come back home, free of all trouble, but his heart had been overwhelmed by the tragic incident and the questions unanswered about his fate. The same indifferent smile had been apparent on his face, however. The driver had waited for him outside to receive him, and the released man had returned home hiding his aching heart.

He came back to himself again, taking his eyes away from the ceiling.

In the meantime, the elegant writer was in her bedroom, enjoying her travels through history. Zola himself had conveyed the truth to her about his masterpiece, and up to now, she had been unable to communicate it to the professor. He hadn't been ready to listen to her. She thought, perhaps this was the best time to convince the professor of the error he was just about to make. He had to be stopped somehow. The truth had to be revealed, the truth about Julien, Colombel and Thérèse de Marsanne. She made her way to the telephone, picked it up and returned herself to her cozy bed; she was comfortable enough, covered by her blanket. Finally, she was going to say it.

The telephone rang in his home. The boy answered and conveyed to the master that his latest visitor, the girl who wrote, was wanting to speak to him, and she was answered from the extension on his bedside table.

"Sir, I want to tell you…," she said, making a simple effort.

"Yes? Are you going to talk about it again? Your *secret*? And you don't want to tell me? I don't want to know about it."

She was interrupted with the same irritation before she could say anything, as he didn't have the slightest doubt about what she was just about to say. Well, she was silenced again, and she ended up turning her question into another.

"Do you think that Émile Zola really loved that laundress?… I don't think so."

Listening to this most unexpected question, his magnificence declared his sentiments in the most unsupportive way.

"I don't know. He's a dead man. Why bother about someone who's not even living?"

She didn't stop herself at his reply. Covered by her blanket, she found more coziness as she presented her understanding in her next question:

"Is he really dead? No, he's not. He's living."

Her playful tone was very decorative and dressed up her words prettily, but they, unfortunately, held her back from expressing her deeper self. She was an unfortunate soul who never did express herself, and he was all the more unfortunate, never understanding the depth of her words. He didn't understand that she really spoke to the loneliness, deep inside him, and truthfully the monsieur was nowhere in her expressions. It was him, always him, the professor, the gigantic figure in the performing arts. What an excellent finding!

"What do you mean?" he asked, unable to understand her.

She was silent for a while, expressing nothing about her discovery, and then she spoke again, with her blanket tight and warm around her, hiding her sympathetic devotion.

"Is he really dead?" she asked again in the same cheery tone, this time with a slight laugh.

What idiocy she was expressing on the surface when her heart continuously dealt in brilliant understanding!

He asked the next obvious question: "Have you gone out of your mind?"

He certainly thought that she was rejoicing in her own way, just like she always did—or made him believe that she did—and she said nothing. Yes, she could do nothing but merely laugh at his words, encouraging him to confirm that he was right.

"You're just crazy, just gone crazy. He lived more than a century ago."

"No, that's not true. He's living still. He's living! He's living!"

There was laughter on her end, reassuring him further, of her merriment, and so he went on giving weight to his own understanding, which was a sheer misunderstanding.

He turned back to the ceiling, diving into his sorrows.

"Sir, can I get you something to drink?" the boy asked, peeping into his room.

"Tea would do," he said.

The boy went to the kitchen and began to make the master's tea. The master still kept drawing his art on the ceiling or watching the art he had already drawn. It was a movie on the silver screen—enjoyed, loathed and accepted, altogether.

The boy entered, placed the tea on the bedside table and disappeared, glancing at the master's obsession. He loved his master and told himself before he returned to his daily chores that he would never leave him. It wasn't the first time that he convinced himself of it. Knowing nothing about his own inability, the master kept working repetitively on his own artwork, all over the ceiling, never giving a definite answer to his conscience. He couldn't stop the next drawing that was beginning to show its glory.

There had been another questioning, again in the same criminal investigation department, however, about another conflict. It had happened like this:

A leader from the opposition had been visited by gunmen at a time when the world had been in a deep sleep. The brutes had disappeared with aggression, after the threat on continuing any political campaign. So, the questioning had begun with the investigation, and it had happened again in the opposite direction.

"Why am I a suspect in this? What evidence do you have against me?"

"Well, he participated in the political campaign of your opposition and spoke against your leader."

"Is that sufficient enough? Just because he's in the opposition, I'd threaten him by sending gangsters to his house?"

The police had continued the questioning, but it had ended in the same manner, with not enough evidence against him.

He returned to himself again, sipping his tea, not knowing that he was making the boy, who was checking on his master regularly, very happy. This time, the young boy disappeared for a long time with the false understanding that the master had settled down, but really the master was making more drawings on the ceiling, one after the other.

He took the article again into his hand and gasped at another highlight, about another questioning and then another and another. In all the interrogations of the official investigations, there had been one common error: insufficient evidence. Hence, he had been released. It was hard for anyone to say, even with the highest mindreading skills, if he was really involved in the crimes. His face gave no sign, and his eyes gave no indication at all. His agony was never apparent in him. Reading his eyes was the hardest thing to do, so he grieved, silently grieved, in isolation.

Suddenly he saw flames, flames of a museum burning down to ashes and the allegations after. However, all charges had ended in futility with a smooth release, leaving him to answer his conscience, and of course, that was where the final verdict waited for him with open arms. But again, no one could fathom his guilt or innocence. Only he knew it, and he divulged it to the girl who wrote his untold story, through his own description of the greatest French novelist, Émile Zola.

At this time, quite a distance away from him in her little home, she was reading the same article, all wrapped up in her blanket. It looked like the content really didn't matter to her. However, she wondered if he could be capable of such devastation, and she was well fixed to the underlining of the inconsistent, ephemeral human mind, where nothing was permanent or everlasting.

Suddenly, she felt warm. Yes, she wasn't in a chill anymore, and she realized that she had been sweating for some time. So, the blanket was taken away and thrown to a side, before she stood up and made her way to the balcony again. Yes, there was the same lonely star still in the sky, opening up her heart to the same stream of thoughts. How vast the sky was! How massive the lonely planet was! And how trivial she was!

She still held hands with the lovely dressmaker, who had tried to tell the monsieur about the men she had encountered. He hadn't given any good ear to her, making her disheartened, so she decided to lie low about it. Perhaps he already knew about spies being around, as he drew the political attention of the time.

The monsieur was still watching young Thérèse in the balcony, who was sending kisses to the sky, giving a blind eye to the disturbance behind the tree. But it didn't mean that she didn't observe it. She felt the movements behind the tree with all her senses. The monsieur, confident in his hiding place, still had his thoughts fully open, wondering how indifferent a woman could be after condemning two lively men to death, whether purposefully or incidentally. Was it female domination over male domination, or was it merely the wonderful craft of a sexually dominating woman, just for a night of love? It was left to be answered.

Thérèse was totally into the sky, making the great writer think that she was absolutely nothing except what she appeared to be. He made the best out of her obsession and pulled his bicycle away from the tree, in an attempt to withdraw himself. He had no doubt about his hiding place in the dark, as she had her whole being concentrated on the sky.

Slowly, the bicycle moved backwards and then to a side. It reached the road with the happy rider, happy to disappear without being noticed. He got onto the bicycle but looking back and seeing the viciousness up there, he realized that he had been hoodwinked. By then, beautiful Thérèse de Marsanne had left the sky and come back down to the balcony and had begun to dive on earth. She had the observer fully in her sight before she released him with a malicious smile. And he began to ride his bicycle faster than usual.

He passed the countryside and entered his grounds sooner than he expected, knowing well that there was a lovely, waiting for him somewhere far now, in her own home. He was determined to visit her, no matter how far she lived. There was no doubt that she hadn't yet fallen asleep.

Jeanne was there diving in the sky, still trying to find a star. She looked worried, waiting for the monsieur, gazing at the road from time to time. She had expected him to come down the road directed to the country, and not at all from the other side, so she didn't see him when he really came. He stood in a way to be seen by her, and it happened very quickly. She was happy. Was it going to take a long time, his most anticipated entrance? No, not really.

He stood at a distance, and she still watched him through the window. No emergence happened this time, no breaking of bars. It was his turn now. He kept looking through her for some time with a slight smile on his face. In a while, he walked into the house, and she turned back to her room, closing the window behind. She admired her pretty face in the mirror and began to wander in her room. Her heart was dealing with its most intense longing.

On the other end, the monsieur was in his element. He was a loner, a stranger in his own home, so he had no limitations. In no time, Jeanne rose to the knock on her door. She opened the door, and he walked in.

19th–20th Century

Zola spent his life between the two cities, Alexandrine and Jeanne. The latter, the seamstress, was making dresses from home now. It was a home trade. There was a senior seamstress, Adeline, who worked with her.

Jeanne had loads of sewing to do. Of course, this was her new home on the surface, and her obscure home was the man she loved. By then, Alexandrine had come to know about her husband's *other wife*, Jeanne, the seamstress who lived in another town now. She also knew about his frequent visits to her. Although she vehemently disapproved of it at first, she gradually began to comply with it later.

Apart from his concentration on Thérèse de Marsanne, Julien and Colombel, with their incredible story of one night's love which eternally haunted him, Zola had another concern: his liberated effort to save his friend, Dreyfus, the very reason he was the nation's centre of attention, the very reason he had spies following him.

Dreyfus was a French artillery officer who was on trial, and his conviction created unrest in the country, resulting in an aggressive political drama. He was convicted as a war criminal, a traitor who gave information about new artillery parts to the rival army. The Dreyfus Affair resulted in an eruption in the society, and he was degraded in a court-martial, before consecutive life imprisonment in Devil's Island. The onlookers watched as he disappeared behind bars, leaving a memory in their hearts and confirming his innocence in very firm words as he cried out:

"I swear that I am innocent. I remain worthy of serving in the army. Long live the army!"

His words were carved in Zola's mind, and they could never be erased. He began his work with extreme enthusiasm. He was a great writer who sat down in his library with his pen, his only weapon. He started his excellent piece of writing, the open letter to the president of the country which he kept publishing in the newspaper.

J'Accuse…!
Lettre Au Président de la Republique….

He began and went on for pages and pages, every week, never failing with it at any time. There were times that it created more conflict than when Dreyfus was convicted with denial of pardon, but it didn't discourage Zola, the great writer, the man of esteem who knew that he was right, who had very high regard for all opinions but always worked with his own. What else could be expected from a man of that esteem, who lived out loud?

His letter to the president started with politeness, affirmation, and insistence.

Sir,

Would you allow me, grateful as I am for the kind reception you once extended to me, to show my concern about maintaining your well-deserved prestige and to point out that your star, which until now has shone so brightly, risks being dimmed by the most shameful and indelible of stains?

He was taking his own extended time, putting his words on paper. The words were questioning, affirming and exclaiming, not giving any idea to the reader about his misery, when he was in the process of writing it. A little sparrow came flying to his window and perched on the sill, reminding him of his forgotten past again, haunting him, treasured and remembered always. And further away behind the bird, he heard his innocent friend's cries of anguish. He saw him trapped in the secret court-martial and the agony that followed, so he took his pen back to his sturdy grip.

When he was beginning to write about the guilty parties, he heard a slight sound at the door, and it disturbed him.

"I've brought a warm drink to you, monsieur." Jeanne entered with a smile, expecting to give the warmest consolation to his heart that constantly grieved.

"Why are you here?" he asked, giving maximum weight to his words.

The pretty seamstress, the pure heart, stopped at his tone as she was frightened.

"I haven't asked for anything! You didn't have to come here! Be with your own work and don't come here again!" the monsieur firmly stated, very sure of his words.

The tender soul was stunned and had no strength to speak a word at the unforeseen reaction of the man who possessed her heart. She withdrew herself and quickly disappeared behind the door. Her legs became light, and she almost fell down on her way but did her best to keep up. She succeeded in keeping her head up until she stopped. It was done, and she sat down again with her sewing. That was where she belonged, and there was no doubt about it now. She looked at her hands, which trembled along with her fingers and her whole frame, as she took up the sewing materials. She dropped them again from her shaking hands. Was he in some kind of a peculiar situation? Was that the reason he behaved in such an unusual manner? Perhaps he was fully engaged with some outstanding work and didn't tolerate any disturbance.

With her hands quivering, she looked at the outfits left to be ironed and decided that she should switch to them. The iron took her with full force, and she had no escape from it, so she began her work, having visions of a lovely girl's dilemma, someone who lived more than a century in the future. How remarkable! Their eyes met.

Meanwhile, the monsieur was building his dwelling in his newspaper article, his letter to the president, expressing to the best of his knowledge and skills, his accusations of the guilty parties of the Dreyfus case, doing his best to prove his friend's innocence. His pen was doing excellent work, succeeding over any kind of weapon. His arguments—strong, wired with the underlined evidence, crystal clear—didn't leave any questions. He didn't spare anyone in his accusations, triumphing in his efforts to prove the innocence of wrongfully accused Dreyfus. His accusations, strong and sharp, were plentiful, not on one party but on many. He strongly accused military individuals, law officials and even religious organizations that were responsible for the false charges against Dreyfus; he believed firmly that the president had to be informed.

Jeanne, further away, was still shaken by the thunder that had struck her. She couldn't fathom any reason for his anger, but she tried to understand; it was the same effort that she was going to reap one day. She slowly tiptoed to him once again, in between her work, making sure that he didn't see her. She was hesitant when she came closer, wanting to run away from the sudden memory of his fury, but she stayed and moved forward slowly, making sure that she made no sound.

She stopped at the door, taking extra precautions not to make any noise this time, and she was happy at her success. From the edge of the door, she could see him, in the same position, turned towards the window with his thoughts far away. But it looked like he was done with his work. His pen was resting on the table with a pile of papers, having fully completed his letter. It had to be some important work then if he was that furious at the disturbance that came in the middle of it. Jeanne knew it, although she had no idea what it really was.

Darkness was going to fall soon, and Jeanne got lost in her room, giving much thought to the depth of the night. She stood by the window watching outside, at the thickness of the darkness and the shiny planets in the sky. Her curly hair was blowing in the wind and falling down until her waist, giving her a very casual look. Concentrating intensely on the sky, she almost forgot to blink her eyes, which didn't differ much from the stars that shined there. Her bright eyes gave clear evidence of a pure heart that longed for her devotion.

She turned back to the room, which looked exactly the same before she began her travel among the planets far away. The door to the room stood at a distance, with no promise of his entrance. She thought it would happen at any time, or perhaps it would never happen. However, she waited, together with her unstained heart.

She turned back to the sky, admiring its beauty again and also recognizing her triviality, confirming within herself that the tiny stars were massive planets. Oh, how beautiful—among the stars, she could see a face, a very familiar face that belonged to the future, that waited ahead of her; it was the face of a writer, a writer of a dressmaker and her virtue, a writer of herself and her devotion.

They met with their eyes in silent smiles. What a significant identification! They read each other deeply. But only one of them wrote:

the one in the sky, the excellent writer, the writer of parallelism. The young dressmaker looked into the writer's eyes in depth. She was dazzled by the tiny pupils that spoke to her with a sparkle left in them. Simultaneously, the viewer's bright eyes were weighed by the one in the sky. They had plenty for each other.

Jeanne turned back to her room and glanced at the door again, which was still silent with no clue of being opened by her most awaited guest. It looked like he was going to take the longest time in the world, so she returned to the sky to meet the lovely association again, confirming clearly that she was longed for, by her. The one up there looked disappointed when Jeanne turned away, and happily accepted her return. They embraced each other wholeheartedly, in recognition, identification, and understanding, although with no proper realization. It happened in a quick moment, and Jeanne had to leave her passion at a sudden sound behind, making the beauty in the sky slowly disappear.

She turned her head quickly to the door, accepting his arrival. She wanted to ask him why he had been in a terrible state of anger that evening, but he spoke way before she thought he would.

"Please don't disturb me in the library!" His words were very stern again. They made her speechless, just like they had done earlier. He didn't leave her any room to express herself.

She maintained silence, unable to make the slightest movement to voice herself, and most significantly, trying to understand the temperament in front of her. She loved him, and it was that love, treasured deep within, that accepted, invited and endured him.

The door was locked behind in no time, and they soon found each other's souls.

More nights were spent in the same heartfelt eagerness, she waiting for him in the dark, the major figure in political liberty, the most wonderful lover. How fascinating! Only a handful knew about the unexposed passion of the controversial novelist, towards the young seamstress.

Jeanne used to visit the church every Sunday, and she heard many stories about the monsieur and his work concerning his letter to the president, on the Dreyfus Affair. Having heard some severe criticisms, she tried to come to her own assumptions about them, but with little understanding. Whatever her opinion was, the condemnations worried her to the same level.

"Zola is trying to defend him because they're good friends."

"He just has no proof to support his innocence."

"He's got his own personal reasons for defending him."

She attempted to give a deaf ear to what she heard although it was a futile exercise. She didn't even know the perfection in them whatsoever. Among the many critics, there were also her friends, and sometimes she wished she could ask them, question them, and get to know the truth from them, but she was hesitant. She was worried that they might notice her susceptibility, that they might know that she had some other reason in addition to the obvious keenness anyone would have.

One day, it so happened when she was in the marketplace that she heard a very interesting piece of dialogue.

"The case will go up to the president now. Zola's done a marvellous work."

"Why is he trying to defend Dreyfus when he's proved of treason? He's convicted of giving out information."

"It's not him. It's not Dreyfus. All responsible parties are mentioned in his letter."

"This man has something up his sleeve."

"No, he's just honest and very straightforward."

"How can you be sure that he's right?"

"Zola's not a man who'd speak out if he didn't have any evidence."

Jeanne heard them very clearly, and she drew herself closer while another man joined the fascinating conversation.

"He absolutely has no evidence, it's only his predictions and assumptions doing the work. Look what he always does, just shouts out loud for everything. That's all."

"He's crazy to do it if he didn't really know, if he didn't have any proof."

The lovely argument came to a sudden stop, at the noise that clashed in the middle of it, drawing the entire street. The town was in total unrest while the demonstration followed.

"Hail to Dreyfus! Long live the army! Long live our motherland!"

The street's eyes turned towards the protest with all their senses on, and the arguers had nothing else to do but watch, while Jeanne, too, had all her curiosity at work. It was a large parade and quite an outburst with an endless uproar.

"Long live Zola! The voice of justice! Bring justice to Dreyfus!"

Jeanne was extremely excited and wished she could take part in it. The words she heard in the background uplifted her enthusiasm, and she ended up hurrying her feet back. On her way, she could hear more words.

"Zola has done some wonder, stimulated people to bring justice to Dreyfus."

"Justice to a traitor?"

"He's no traitor. Real traitors are just free out there."

"An innocent man's behind bars."

"Zola, I know, will work on it until he's proved innocent."

She extended her ears to everything she could take while rushing back; some of them sounded like sweet honey. She loved it when the monsieur was praised, whether he was right or wrong. Yes, she didn't really know how true or untrue their words were, and she wasn't even worried about their accurateness. No matter how accurate or inaccurate they were, she loved him, and that was her only concern. But she decided to ask him, ask him the truth about what she heard, not so much for any need of an underlined sentence, but she just wanted to know, for the sake of understanding and for the desire of asking him.

She was obsessed by her new home where the monsieur frequently visited, and her whole involvement was, of course, being his *other wife*, his current conflict and how far he was involved in it, more than anything, how disturbed he was. She returned home, and it didn't take a long time for her to return to sewing and ironing. Being well prepared for just about anything, she settled down with the steam iron.

It took a long time, and she had finished most of it when the monsieur walked in with some of his clothing. It was a sudden entrance which made her happy; the man she loved was there in front of her. How she did love him! She wished she could run into his arms and feel them. When they were busy placing his outfits, she wished she could crawl under his arms and tell him that he did the righteous thing, fighting for the liberation of Dreyfus. Yes, he was right. The world might have said that he made statements with no proof. Yes, they might have said, a traitor himself would help another traitor, but she was going to stand by him and say that he was never one.

But soon he disappeared without even really noticing her, although he knew that she was there. She was disappointed by the indifference he showed. He wasn't paying any attention to her or so she thought.

She decided to ask him about the unrest in town, the conflict that involved him; she wanted him to say it, without hiding anything in his heart that might burst one day. Yes, that was the best choice, at least for now, even if she still didn't know— besides the fact that they frequently met—if she had the right to ask him about it or anything else. She kept thinking while her hands were busy with the steam tool. It worked mechanically on all the outfits, and there were only a few to do now.

He entered again.

The number of outfits still left to be done irritated him, and he swiftly turned his eyes towards her.

"Why are they still here undone? It's irritating when things aren't done on time," he said, directing his insistence on her.

She was nervous, and with trembling hands, she held the iron tight as she spoke.

"Monsieur, I didn't know, didn't know that…"

"Didn't know what?"

"That you wanted them soon."

"How can it be? When I've given them to you, left them here, isn't it clear that I need them?"

He worded this in the toughest tone, and the young dressmaker was astonished. Her weak hands were trembling, unable to keep a proper grip on the iron; she let it fall on her feet. She picked it up in a flash and started her work again, and the monsieur, seeing the little accident she had, fell into a deeper fury, one mingled with love. He quickly ended up helping her in the little accident.

"Is that how you do your job? The iron won't be stable in your hand?"

The girl was more disturbed at his words, although she was being charmed in his arms.

"I'm sorry, monsieur. It'll be done soon," she softly whispered.

He vanished behind the door in a while. She had tears pouring down her cheeks, but with great effort, she drew them back to her eyes. The work was done, and she thought it was best to transfer the ironed outfits to him. Perhaps this would be the right time to find answers to the confusion built up in the marketplace. But perhaps, it wasn't the best time for such questions, as he was in the highest level of temper.

She reached him, carrying his outfits, while he was standing at the window, looking outside. He didn't make the slightest turn at the sound of her entrance. She placed the well folded attire on the shelf and hung the rest, well organized.

The monsieur was still facing the opposite. Jeanne tiptoed towards him with only one purpose: touching and soothing his wounded heart with every intention of healing it. But, hesitant, she stood awhile just a few steps behind him, wondering, holding herself carefully. Then, little by little, she stepped towards him, feeling the fingers of one hand folded in those of the other, holding them tight in front of her slender waist, a waist that could melt the hardest of rocks and everything except the solidity that stood in front of her: the one and only Émile Zola.

"Monsieur," she whispered.

There was no reaction to her address, so she murmured softly again.

"Monsieur."

This time he ended up making the quickest turn, and she was almost drawn back. She was reluctant again to question those eyes filled with trouble and disturbance, but she knew that her silence would result in a higher fury, so she voiced her bewilderment.

"Monsieur, why do people make such allegations, some against you and some with you? Why are they rioting?"

21st Century

"Sir, I don't want to disturb you, but why has he published this?" she asked.

"So, what can I do? What do you want me to do about it?" he coolly asked.

"Is it true? I just want to know if it's true. Did it really happen?" she asked.

He gave a swift and firm reply. "Lots of people have asked me about it. But, no. It didn't happen."

"So, you didn't do it?"

"No, I didn't."

She could feel nothing but his frankness and sincerity, opened up with genuineness.

"He can't just say things like that about you and go scot-free after slandering you. Something should be done."

He smiled at the young writer's comment and kept quiet for some time, recalling his coincidental meeting with the slanderer after his gorgeous publication.

It had happened at a cultural event in town. There had been a large gathering—the professor, the leading politician and performing artist—being one of the main invitees. The get-together had taken place in a two storeyed building. Among the crowd, he had spotted the slanderer involved in a deep conversation and he, the slanderer, having seen his prey, had begun to be the prey of his prey.

"I met him one day at a function," he said.

"So, what happened, sir?" she most curiously asked.

"When I went there, I saw him talking with some friends."

"So, then?"

"He saw me and couldn't face me."

As he went on explaining, she kept extending her listening senses, resting her face on her hands while he sat right in front of her, in the middle of Thérèse, Julien, and Colombel.

"He was trying to ignore me. He just walked away and started climbing steps to the upper floor, and I followed him."

"Did you, sir? So, what happened afterwards?"

"He was trying his best to hide from me, feeling guilty about what he did. I kept following him until he had no other place to hide. At one point, he had to face me."

"Then what happened, sir?"

"I called out his name and waved my hand, and he had no escape."

"So, what did he do?"

"He waved at me and quickly turned back to his company."

She carefully observed him and his talkativeness, which wasn't really like him. He was with the best person to let go of it all. Yes, the girl who wrote was his best listener now, the one who understood his need to be understood.

"How can he just slander you like that, sir? He can be sued."

"Well, he's just trying to sell his tabloid."

"Let it be sold, but how can he try to become popular by insulting you? That's not fair."

She looked carefully at him as he turned back to his work, exhibiting indifference to the same devastation that he had reacted to, with a rush of emotions. Really, he had a lot more to tell her, but she stopped remarking, and so did he.

The young boy appeared suddenly in front of her eyes, approaching them behind his master with a warm drink served on a tray. Having raised her head at the movement in front of her, she placed her eyes on the young servant, who looked back at her and gave her a pleasant smile, which was instantly returned. He was her silent friend who adored her. His master was looking down still, concentrating on his work, and he made a quick glance at the servant, at his approach. The boy quickly placed the tray on the table and disappeared into the kitchen.

"You can have that," he said, pointing to the drink.

She took it in her hand and began to sip it, although she hated to sip a drink in his presence. Soon she was done. It also looked like she was done with her writing for the day; it was time to leave, so she had nothing to do but disappoint him again.

"Sir, I have to go now," she said.

He still had his head down with no indication of having heard her words. She began to pack her bag, and that disturbed him.

"What are you doing?" he asked.

"I have to go, sir," she said.

His disappointment could be plainly seen in his face, and she became sympathetic. The walls of his home began to feel the same loneliness that would overwhelm him, and he murmured the same words.

"Do you really have to go now?"

She heard her heart weep at his question, and there were psychological rays around her that would extend their hands to assign her there forever, but she had to be detached. There were forces around her that would harm him, and he had to be shielded.

"Yes, sir, it's time to leave," she whispered in her softest voice.

"Don't go now! Stay a little more!"

She heard this, the humblest request, coming from one dominant man. Her whole heart accepted his loneliness with a wide welcome note that neither she nor he could ever imagine. She walked towards him and stood there in front of him. It happened in a moment. She embraced him with both hands. It was a sympathetic embrace, and he rested his heart in her bosom. At a sudden call and recall, she looked around to find the pleasant smiles in the portrait, placed on the most attractive shelf in his home. She recognized her charming smiles. The packed bag was unpacked again, while the softest whispers were spontaneously being relieved from the most delicate girl in the world, one who would cross all barricades to recover him.

"I will, sir," she said. "I will stay."

She wanted to heal and soothe his entire life, throughout his journey.

He watched his fond assistant with dazing eyes, trying his best to draw them back to the papers where Julien, Colombel, and Thérèse were left alone, at least for a moment. And she started writing again. The boy came in, seeking his master's permission to go out and it was given with no delay, allowing him to leave sooner than expected.

The wonderful association began to extend further into each other's arms. Making love with extreme passion, she almost fell on the table. It started in the gentlest manner and eventually began to look like a brawl. Yes, they were in a brawl of making love.

Time passed, and her fear began to rise with the setting of the sun, the fear that tortured her every day, at every second. She had to say it to him, however much she loathed. There was something, a solid fact that was unknown to him which she would or wouldn't make known to him someday. He already had his regrets and griefs so she, the sympathetic soul, had nothing more to do than to shoulder it within.

"Sir, I think I have to go now," she said.

This time, he smiled as he understood her need to return home, but he had no doubt about another reason, except the very evident one that everyone returned home at the end of the day. She packed her bag again and started towards the door, and he accompanied her. He reached the lock first so that he could stop her from unlocking the door. They stood there for some more time unable to let go of each other's arms, but with reluctance, she made her move: she softly and intentionally turned the lock. It gave an abrupt stop to the dominant professor, and he was drawn back. But it happened in a way that she fell in his arms again. He softly reached her lips, and it was the gentlest embrace in the world. They found themselves in each other again, and there was a long silence.

The door was opened again. Being clearly confirmed that they didn't fall in any other's eyes, she reached his arms again for a quick moment, before she disappeared into the elevator. She went all the way down, passing the security point where the guard sat all alone, missing visitors. It was that deserted. She called a trishaw and got onto it as soon as she could, making sure that the world was dazzled by her gleam, so she couldn't be seen. How excellently it was done! Even the driver couldn't properly see her. He stopped at the right house, and she walked in.

She quickly unlocked the door and lost herself inside, reluctant to turn on the lights; she leaned on the door. Closing her eyes, she let him enter her depths with blossoming thoughts. There was no time or need to travel through history, at least for the time being. She was living the present, with the dominant figure, Monsieur Zola, and the very tender girl, Jeanne.

She took a quick shower and changed into her night clothes. Having wrapped herself in her blanket, she had nothing to do but dream of him, his long waits, while he lost himself in his bed picturing her comings and goings. A sudden rain fell on both parties, washing their thoughts away and bringing them to the extreme present. She heard the doorbell and ran to open the door, knowing well who was at the doorstep: the most unwanted. She had no choice now, except open it, to accept her most dreaded scenario. And yes, it was them.

"Where have you been?" a rough voice asked.

They barged in, almost pushing her inside, and she ended up hitting her head on the table. She did her best to stand on her feet.

"I have the right to go where I want. I will do it when I want, and I don't need anyone's permission!" she screamed as loud as she could.

At her stern words, her main visitor, the chief shot himself towards her without losing a single moment and grabbed her hair.

"Since when did you get such audacity in your head?" he asked.

She became very uncomfortable in his sturdy hands and realized that she was in a vain struggle to free herself.

"I'll give you this one chance only. There won't be a next time. In case there is one…"

He paused, meaning the worst and thrust her against the wall, holding her by the neck. She was nothing but a fawn in a tiger's grasp. There was no space around her, and she had nothing to do but wait until she was released. It did happen in a while, the hardest, most aggressive release. She was happy, as it was a release of some sort anyway.

"For now, I'm leaving. But make sure! I'll be back," he muttered in the loudest possible voice.

She had her head down drawing an art on her face with her fingertips. She was hurt, extremely hurt, and her soft fingers did nothing much to soothe her wounds. Yes, there was nothing she could do, except watch while her sudden but frequent visitor walked up to the door and stopped there again before he vanished. He turned around to take a last look at her, his face enriched with a scornful smile, at her struggle to bring herself together. She was breathing hard in fear, feeling herself a dead soul. He disappeared behind the door, slamming it, leaving her in a terrible perplexity mingled with fright.

She ran to the door and locked it, making sure that she was all alone now and there was no one else, for even otherwise, solitude was what she liked. In a flash, she made her way to the balcony to watch her visitors leave, on time to get a clear view of them, as they got into the pickup. The main guest who sat in the front raised his head to look at the balcony before the driver started the vehicle, and seeing her fail, was happy again. The vehicle moved very fast, and she walked back inside, having locked the door, her body hurting and wounds burning.

The kettle was turned on for a hot coffee, which was definitely what she wanted. Quickly making it and pouring it into her mug, she gave her weight to the sofa in her bedroom. She was still not really herself, but fright alone that yearned for comfort. She wanted to call him, her heart's professor, but she was hesitant to make any move to bring her wish into action. She kept sipping her coffee, realizing that she was never going to call him. He would be the last solution sought by the sympathetic girl who would never disturb him with her own conflicts. Yes, she only existed as a source of comfort to him. What a perfect theory! And what else could be expected from such wonderful, excellent understanding? Nothing! Absolutely nothing! She was too compassionate to let it flow on him, being the giver of ease and not the recipient. Was she fair by herself? Wasn't it unfair in every aspect, unfair by him, to keep him in the dark about it? Being already justified, she didn't stop to think about its fairness. The simple, complicated girl was taking all laws into her hands.

The telephone kept inviting her, but, enduring her wounds, she never approached it, no matter how strong the invitation was.

In the meantime, on the other side of the town, the professor had his thoughts finely active. She was extraordinary, different from others; she looked like she was hiding some important fact about herself when she spoke. Also, she continuously told him that she longed to reveal something to him, apparently something of importance, but she was never ready to mention it. What could it be? He tried his best to make the right guess, although none of his assumptions agreed with his own thoughts. How unfortunate! At the other end, she was looking out of the window, comparing her triviality with the immensity of the universe.

There was no end to the sipping of the coffee, and her dread slowly began to vanish away, just like everything else. She had lots to do before the next day about Julien, Colombel, and Thérèse, so she started her usual search through history. There was no end to it, just like always, with Julien coming first sometimes, next Thérèse and occasionally Colombel, a mysteriously beautiful and unforgettable trio. She laughed with them, spoke to them and very often travelled with time to that very dominant figure, Émile

Zola, and the young seamstress, Jeanne Rozerot. She wondered what they would have been doing if they had lived in the present, and every time the question came up in her, she knew that it wasn't really a question at all, for she knew very well that they were idealistically contemporary, living modern.

At one given time, Julien was playing the flute in his little home, outspreading his eyes towards Thérèse's window while Thérèse was in her bedroom with Colombel. She heard the flute and was drawn towards it naturally: the most melodious tune she had ever heard which was harmonious with the climate, the beautiful landscape and everything else out there. Thérèse burst open her window and listened to the music, resting her face on her hands, and lonely Julien was happy. Was she going to throw kisses at him again? Was she going to come down from the balcony and meet him face to face? Was she really in love with him? No question was answered, but he had them making their art in his heart when Colombel appeared right behind her. Julien was stunned by the unexpected appearance of his enemy, but he continued to play the flute, although at his own risk now. Young Colombel had his arms around his sweetheart, and they both disappeared, shattering the rest of Julien's dream. How pathetic!

The obsessed writer was done with her writing. It took a few hours, and she kept all the papers together, in order. It was a thick pile, and she was pleased with its completion. The next day, she was going to hand it over to him, and he was going to be as happy as she was. Oh, what a lot she could do! Yes, she could do much more than she was really doing.

She woke up early morning, and it was time to attend her lectures. The morning session was a brief one, and it was done quickly, faster than she thought it would, ending up in a break of an hour. It was the right time to visit him. She feared to step out, anyway, recalling the incident of the night before, but nothing was going to stop her from reaching him. She came out of the university grounds, her eyes wandering around, scrutinizing every little thing. It looked safe to progress, and the line of trishaws was her best choice. She got into one, and the driver started towards the right address.

The trishaw stopped in front of his apartment building, and she walked in with only a few minutes left. She was sure that she wasn't being watched, and most coincidentally that was when the young servant came out of the elevator and saw her right away. He walked straight towards her, full of smiles.

"What are you doing here? He's not home. He had to go out urgently, some political meeting," he said.

"I see. Are you going for groceries?"

"Yes, just to the marketplace."

"Can I join you?"

The boy was delighted by her request. It made his day, and he jumped at the idea.

"Oh, sure, with pleasure, please join me!" he blurted out.

And they both made their way to the market. She wouldn't have been stopped by the most difficult hurdle in the world, neither by an attacker nor by a threat. This time, she didn't stop to look around. It was an enchanting little visit to the market.

"What do you want to buy?" she asked on her way.

"Some vegetables and other kinds of groceries."

"Oh, that's a good thing, then. I can pick."

"Sure."

"But, don't tell him that I came with you!"

"Okay, sure, I won't tell him."

The couple headed to the market, each holding equal levels of confidence, she with her pleasant dream and he with his eagerness to have his master's visitor as his lovely companion. They entered the market complex, and she was surprised about her own behaviour now, the very same girl who dreaded that there could be a stalker or an attacker, following her.

She followed the boy, paying attention to what he was buying, and he was explaining himself even without her request, as she needed some explanation.

"This is for his morning herbal porridge," he said, picking herbs.

She simply followed him, while listening to him.

"Now, some vegetables. He's not so fond of meat."

The boy went from store to store and bought what he knew was right, and in a while, he was done. Then it was time to pose her question.

"When is he coming back home today? He's getting in late, right?"

"Yes, he's attending a lecture and then rehearsals after the meeting, so it'll be late."

The pair hopped into a trishaw to go home with the heavy bags, even though it was a very short distance. They found themselves in front of the building sooner than expected.

"You can have a ride back home in this trishaw. I completely forgot you're going back home," he said very loudly, as he had to compete with the noise of the busy town.

"But, I'll get down with you," she said.

They both got down. The boy, confused, stayed back for a bit as if to ask her why she got off, knowing very well that his master was absolutely not home, and she had no reason to get down. She understood him and didn't delay in solving his confusion.

"Will you keep it a secret if I tell you something?" she asked.

"Okay, another secret! What?" he asked with a smile.

The boy was taken by her fun-loving nature, which excellently concealed her inner agony. She took advantage of his smiles, which flashed upon her from time to time, and hid her burns within; they covered the sores that would have been apparent.

"Let's get going inside, first!" she said.

They both walked into the elevator and reached his home. He locked the door, and she sat down, ready to express herself. The young boy was still standing in front of her, giving her plenty of time, and at last, she spoke.

"I'm going to be the chef today!"

The words were blurted out in the same playful tone, and the young boy gave out a laugh, full of delight.

"I'm so happy," he said.

"Really? Why?" she asked.

"An excellent writer is going to make dinner tonight."

"Excellent writer? How do you know? Have you read anything I've written?"

"No, I haven't read, but he said."

"Did he? What did he say?"

"He told me that he only needs to tell you a few words and you end up writing everything he's been thinking, everything in his heart."

19th–20th Century

Political unrest was at its highest and Jeanne was distressed more than anyone else, purely because of the monsieur's involvement in it, with his efforts to prove the innocence of Dreyfus. She heard about it in the churchyard, in the marketplace and almost everywhere she went. She had once asked him the truth about it, but no proper answer had been given. Perhaps he thought that she didn't really have to know anything about it, or he didn't have to mention it to her. However, Jeanne was most concerned, and there was no end to her concentration on him.

She hated anti-Dreyfusards, and she loved Dreyfusards simply because she wanted to be his helping hand, even if she could do nothing, not even discuss it with him. Point blank, she had no interest in this whole affair of Dreyfus, but she was on the side of the Dreyfusards for the only reason there could be for a simple, ordinary girl.

Once, Jeanne was coming home after Sunday prayers, and a lovely conversation fell in her ears when she was walking across the churchyard.

"Now it's going to be hard for Zola. He's spoken ill of the army, and the army's not going to keep quiet."

"But he's told the truth. His arguments make it clear."

"That's not the problem. Whether it's true or false, now that he's openly said that the army has unjustly convicted Dreyfus, that's enough for his prosecution."

"What do you mean prosecution?"

"Zola's prosecution."

"He's on trial?"

"Yes, for accusing the army of their wrong conviction."

Jeanne, feeble, almost collapsed when she heard the conversation, and she wanted to vanish from there. She hadn't known that he was already on trial for the accusations he had made in the newspaper. Because of her sudden bewilderment after listening to the devastating conversation, she almost lost her way when going home. She was dazzled by the flames of the sun on her way, but she somehow rested herself against a tree, so that she didn't fall down.

She stayed with her back resting on the same tree for some time, in dread, visualizing him being subject to imprisonment and wondering what she could do about it by her tender self, although she knew strikingly well that she could do nothing. She slowly slid herself down so that she could sit down and relax under the tree. And, quite unknowingly, in a while, she went into a slumber, not knowing that she was followed by the same men who had once violently encircled her, who appeared to be secret agents. They were keeping track behind her on her way home from church. Jubilant to find her on a lonely road, they were well focused when they saw her resting down against a tree. Now, she could be approached. She was the best way of reaching Zola.

Far away, totally unaware of the company surrounding her, Jeanne was dreaming the monsieur, in prison. What a horrible life he had there! And how he was tortured! Briskly, she moved ahead to the future where she saw a professor and a girl who wrote, mourning over his imprisonment. She could fully identify them. The former was lamenting over his own plight, which went parallel with the monsieur's, and the latter was grieving over the professor's state and his constant comparison of himself with the historical figure. This was a slumber that was sealed to the future and Jeanne was a significant participant in it. She kept her hands on a piece of art done by the girl in the future. It was wonderful.

He who is lonesome in the crowd sees thee,
Indeed, sees thee and thy lonely self,
Unable to fathom the affection which yields,
Drowns himself in the blissful sea.

The monsieur was in great misery, all by himself and no one else around him. He was in prison—a death sentence. Something horrible was going to happen. She had to hurry. Something had to be done.

She quickly woke up from her dream and stood up on her feet to meet her companions face to face. She hadn't expected to be surrounded by unknown men in a deserted place. She couldn't move ahead. Her frightened eyes gave them some kind of pleasure. She guessed that they were his enemies, anti-Dreyfusards. Perhaps she was right. The men stood scattered, giving her room to walk, but she knew that it was only a trick. However, she started to walk until she came to a dead end, facing another group of men. She turned back to meet the original group and realized that she was fixed to where she stood. They all had the same mockery on their faces.

"What do you want?" Frightened, she broke the silence.

"Zola. And everything about Zola."

She was alarmed by the words thrown at her, although she knew what their requirement was. A few seconds later, one man slowly walked towards her and stopped right in front of her face.

"His plans and whereabouts, that's what we want. From today, you're working for us. And by no means should he know it. If he does … if he does, you know what will happen to him?"

Jeanne became more frightened at his words. The man stood in the same spot as if he expected some kind of an answer from her. She was silent, anyway. She dreaded him too much to speak, but he spoke again.

"Let's meet again here on your next church day?"

It was a question, but he received no answer from her. The girl was looking down in utter fright, and he moved away from her, thus letting her go this time.

She didn't take a long time to speed up her feet again. Across fields and along roads she hurried, fixing her frightened self together, and in a brief time, she was back again in her cozy little home doing the same bit of work, sewing and, of course, ironing, but her dread-filled heart was somewhere else. Work was being done with more concentration and speed. Adeline walked in with some more work, more outfits to iron, breaking her concentration at regular intervals.

Jeanne very well knew that the monsieur was wholly involved in his personal war. It was a war that he fought alone to clear an innocent victim, and it was much more effective and stronger than the constant fight carried on by the Dreyfusards, he was not involved in, whatsoever. Sometimes, it looked like his own conviction. Yes, it did. He was the one who was wrongfully accused, not Dreyfus. That was how dedicated he was in the whole affair, taking it as his own as if it had nothing to do with Dreyfus.

He walked into the sewing room to pick his attire, and of course, he was in a hurry, not even taking a moment to look at the pretty, dread-filled face that was right there in his presence. In truth, he didn't even see her. He picked up his clothes and exited the room, just like that, leaving her to contemplate and make her own speculations.

He was returning to his *first wife*, preoccupied with his own singular focus. Jeanne feared to ask him anything about it, thinking that her questioning would do nothing but disturb him more; she decided not to divulge anything about the incident on her way home from the church. However, she was disturbed by his silence. What could she do, except watch, wait and accept what would come on her way? Or perhaps she was wrong. Perhaps he was silent because he thought that she wasn't concerned. Actually, that was the fact. Both parties were in the same misunderstanding, one misunderstanding the other. It was a mutual misunderstanding. The monsieur was, of course, disturbed, and his behaviour was gradually changing as a result of being totally dedicated to the Dreyfus Affair—which ended up being his own affair—but he never missed out time with his *other wife*. Also, he was eager to discuss with her, his present involvement that caused severe unrest. But she was led by her self-determined unimportance, and she never asked him about it. She thought the one time she really asked him about the problem was sufficient enough, for he didn't show any interest then.

She watched him, thinking of following him, as he walked out of the sewing room, but she didn't. She thought that it would irritate him. However, she walked up to the door and watched him disappear into the hallway. Being left alone with her heavy heart, there was nothing that she could do.

She turned back to the sewing machine; it looked like some kind of life now, and she hoped that she would at least be able to take something from it, but she failed. Just then, she was struck by someone who stood behind her; it was a friendly pat on the shoulder, but she felt it like a drastic gunshot, as it happened at an unexpected moment. Standing up in a swift motion, she ended up resting her head on Adeline's shoulder, weeping aloud, pushing Adeline to a deep level of confusion. Also, she indirectly determined her lament, although it was a simple misunderstanding. Adeline thought that her sudden appearance had given a terrible shock to Jeanne, and she was weeping because she couldn't bear the anxiety of it. But the little dressmaker was lamenting for the monsieur, for his involvement in the political conflict and the imprisonment to come, so she believed. Most of all, she dreaded the enemies that were continuously behind him; perhaps he never knew they existed, or he knew all the time, but never took any notice of them.

"Oh, don't cry! It's only me. Did I frighten you? I didn't mean that. I only came here to talk to you. We haven't spoken much for some time," Adeline said trying to pacify her.

Jeanne was the more capable one and took full advantage of Adeline's misunderstanding. What else could she do? To let her know that she was weeping for the monsieur, thinking that he would face imprisonment? To tell her that she feared that he would be destroyed by his enemies? Never! She had to hide from the world that she was that sensitive to it.

"Oh, I was frightened. I didn't even know that you were here until you stood behind me. I got so scared, so scared," she said, weeping even louder, this time.

"My, my, you can cry until you come out of that shock. I know, I shouldn't have just walked in to startle you. I should have knocked."

The more Jeanne went ahead with the false pretence of being utterly startled by Adeline, the more she was positively misunderstood and the more she gained from it, so she just let the misunderstanding take effect, resting herself on Adeline's shoulder much longer than she really wanted to. Really speaking, that was one way of letting go of her agony, that the other party knew nothing about. She kept weeping until she was ready to return to her work, but it wasn't going to happen. She was never going to be ready. She knew it, so she raised her head before Adeline understood the real reason or before she got the slightest thought that there could be any other reason for her unusual behaviour.

"I have to wash my face," she said, rushing out of the sewing room.

She ran to the sink, opened the water tap and washed her face as much as she could, trying her best to clear her heart. But it was a failure. She could only wash her tears away and nothing else. Her grieving heart remained the same. The towel, hung right next to the sink, helped her to wipe her face and she returned to the sewing room to find her company still waiting there for her. She was making a serious attempt to smile, and Adeline broke the silence.

"Are you feeling good now?"

"Yes," Jeanne replied with the same smile, or rather, in an attempt to smile.

"You got really frightened, didn't you? I didn't mean to frighten you like that."

"It was just unexpected. I'm okay now."

There was a brief time of silence, and Adeline spoke again.

"Oh, what will happen to him at the trial?"

Jeanne was startled by her friend's sudden comment. Knowing that Adeline referred to the monsieur, she remained silent, giving her more time to speak.

"Fighting to bring justice to Dreyfus! Published a letter to the president in *L'Aurore*! Now that it's proved that he was right in his accusations, the army is playing on it. Horrible!"

Adeline kept gazing at Jeanne, trying to gather from her face if she was disturbed by her words, and Jeanne continued her work while extending her ears.

"If it's been proved, then why should he appear in court? Well, the army is still keeping all the evidence without giving them out, so it's not going to work, anyway."

Jeanne was trying very hard to keep her mind at work, but Adeline didn't look like she was going to give up.

"He again accused the army of withholding evidence, and the army has now sued him for libel."

There was a long pause, and she spoke again.

"That's terrifying. So, what will happen? He might be charged, might receive a sentence of imprisonment."

This time, Jeanne was strikingly alarmed, and she burst out her words.

"Imprisonment?"

"Yes, it won't be a very long one. I think it'll be about a year. That's what he's been told, maximum. But he hasn't received it yet. Perhaps tomorrow when he appears in court he'll get to know."

Jeanne came to a startling silence. How could she be this blind to what was going to happen to him, and how could he keep it away from her to this extent? Was he that indifferent to her existence and her love? Did she not know that she was this worried? Was she not anywhere in him? She was overwhelmed by her own assumptions, and from far away she heard Adeline again. She remembered the dreadful encounter on her way home from church and thought perhaps imprisonment was better than going to the hands of enemies. But who were those men? Were they from the army or from some legitimate organization that she knew nothing about? Did it mean that he had no escape, anyway? Her mind was a well-organized muddle.

"I'm going to take these clothes now."

Adeline left with the clothes in her hands when Jeanne was just about to pose her next question, but she was delayed and couldn't utter a word. She sat down, trying to figure out what might happen at his upcoming trial, although it had just been clearly explained to her. She walked to the door trying her best to ask more questions, thinking of bursting them out at Adeline, in the hallway, but she did nothing except let her disappear and watch her walk away.

She turned back and started walking in her room, anxiously, with nothing else to do, wondering what she should be doing. Soon, the day would end. She got lost in her bedroom. She walked to the window and watched the darkness outside. Quite unnoticeably, time was passing at a very rapid speed. She had no control over it, although she was making a futile effort to do so. She looked at the sky, hoping to find a known face from the future, but today there was no trace of her. She was left alone. She saw a lonely star and thought it was perhaps a closer planet, much closer to her. However, all that she could feel was the only fact existing beyond her own thoughts: her insignificance.

Having looked at the time, she turned back to her room, knowing that he wasn't going to see her that night. But she still waited, hoping for the best, expecting him at any time. She opened the door to find no trace of him. Disappointed, she went to bed.

Meanwhile, in another town far away, the monsieur was in his own personal seminar with Thérèse, Colombel, and Julien. They were his favourite creations, and he wasn't really sure of meeting them again, nor was he certain if he had ever brought them to light. But he was giving life to them for the last time. He prepared them, decorated them and made them ready for the future.

It was this:

Thérèse was waiting for Colombel, and neither of them knew that it would be their last meeting. Colombel entered the Marsanne from the same rear door he always did. That way, he knew that he wasn't going to be seen by anyone. She, the wondrous woman, waited for him like she did every night. She had been having very active thoughts first but had begun to be submissive. Circumstances looked like they were changing. She was falling in love with him, although that wasn't at all what she wanted.

At the sudden tune of the flute, she walked up to the window and opened it to see Julien playing his flute. She walked to the balcony and placed her eyes on him, obsessed, and as usual, he misunderstood her, dreaming of her obsession to be with him and nowhere else. The monsieur, too, focused his eyes on him while he played the flute, unable to move them anywhere else. Thérèse knew the working of Julien's mind and enjoyed it like she always did, wanting to tease him. She waved her hand at him. He was thrilled but didn't give up the flute. He admired her golden hair glowing in the moonlight but could hardly see her face. She turned back as she heard the door, and it was Colombel.

In a while, they were in each other's arms, and Julien could slightly see inside the bedroom. He could see their shadows as they moved. He became envious and couldn't bear to see them anymore. The music stopped abruptly, and the lovers inside were disturbed. Detached from each other, they quickly walked to the balcony to find the miserable man, still staring at them. He was definitely saddened but focused on the lovers, who teased him.

Their laughter echoed in his ears, and he was even more depressed. The monsieur felt as if Julien was coming to himself. He tried hard and escaped him. It wasn't hard to do as he was more concerned about his incredible art. Julien, worried, unable to tolerate their laughter, walked inside and shut the door behind him, leaving the lovers up on the balcony, all by themselves.

The young lovers locked themselves inside, and now their shadows could be seen in the dim light very clearly. Julien couldn't help but keep watching them, making sure that they couldn't see him. He turned off the lights of his little home for the same reason. They were making love; their shadows were clearly speaking of their lively spirits. Julien took his eyes away from them, turned his head and lost himself in his bed. What else could be expected from a harmless man like him?

However, there was definitely more to what he could see, and of course, it didn't fall into his senses. The lovely couple up there were challenging each other, one in an unsuccessful attempt to outdo the other. Julien was burning in flames in his bed. Up there, he assumed, was a remarkable duo that broke his heart, shattering his dream.

A few more minutes passed in the same predicament and he raised his head to an unexpected sound. He wondered what it could be. Muddled, he stretched his senses to the bedroom and realized that there was a strange silence now. The room was quiet, and nothing was moving inside. He got off his bed and looked sharply at it, confused.

He walked out of his little dwelling and saw Thérèse on the balcony. She smiled at him, lifting his confusion to its maximum, as it wasn't the same mocking smile that she always gave him. She looked sincere and friendly. So, poor Julien was happy, dreaming again. Not even the slightest thought about Colombel came to his mind, ever. Why was she alone now? What would have happened to Colombel who was with her just a little while ago?

Thérèse began the same little tale. She kissed her soft fingertips and threw the kisses at him, confusing him even more. His eyes stopped at her face. In a while, she continued the process with both hands, and innocent Julien looked around to see if Colombel had come down and Thérèse was really communicating with him. But no, Colombel was nowhere to be seen. She was speaking to no one else but to Julien. He was now out of his dwelling, and all that he wanted was to escape, run away from her and never go back inside.

He began to walk away but couldn't go very far. She had descended without making him notice, and it didn't take her long to catch up with him.

"Come!" she said, holding his hand.

Puzzled, he made an unsuccessful attempt to run away even faster than before.

"Come!" she said again. "Not there! Come here with me! Come! Let's go up there!"

Julien thought that he was dreaming and none of this was true. In a blink, he forgot about Colombel's existence and began to follow Thérèse, she holding his hand in a very tight grip so that he could never escape.

The monsieur looked into the darkness falling in pieces outside. There were no sparrows to be seen out there. It was too dark for the birds. He quickly returned to his creation, steadily grasping every word he wrote years before.

Up in Thérèse's bedroom, Julien almost collapsed, upon seeing the dead body of Colombel, hidden in Thérèse's bed, and she began her fantastic deal.

"I love him," she said. "I love him more than words could ever say. This was just an accident. But I can't have him in here for long. I need your help to take his body from here."

Her words were soft, and she spoke slowly. Julien stayed flabbergasted, not knowing what his next move should be. But Thérèse was making a wonderful promise in return for the favour: one night's love. What a brilliant trade coming from a first-class trader! Just for one night's love with her, he was going to help the beautiful girl remove her lover's dead body! Harmless Julien was provoked. He carried the dead body, hurrying down the steps, not knowing what was going to happen on his way to the lake. Colombel, believed to be dead, would wake up. The unexpected fight between the two men would make them fall, leaving Thérèse alone.

The great writer finished evaluating his masterpiece and left it in the library, thinking of nothing else but the following day and his appearance in the court. He knew more than anyone else what his penalty would be for accusing the army of hiding the evidence that would prove the innocence of Dreyfus. He was ready for it. There was nothing else he could do except avoid imprisonment. He had completed his fine analysis for the future professor of performing arts and the girl who wrote. But, he communicated something else to the future girl, the writer, something different from his original art, and it was excellently grasped by her. And so, he stood up.

Far away in another town, Jeanne was in her bed trying to fall asleep. She knew that he wasn't going to come that night and she couldn't fall asleep, no matter how she struggled.

In his room, he was ready to flee. No court appearance was going to happen.

21st Century

"Sir, this is something important. I have to tell you this." She spoke in the same gentle tone, holding the receiver closer to her lips.

She was delighted about her little adventure, her journey to the history, and wondered whether she would be able to communicate the real story of *Pour Une Nuit D'Amour* to the professor, at least now. The night had done wonders, and she understood the significance made from a century ago. The artist himself had fruitfully communicated to her, and she had to let the professor know about the real story of Julien, Colombel, and Thérèse. However, she wondered if he would ever let her. He didn't even know that he had eaten the dinner made by her. In fact, she had made the boy promise her to keep it a secret. However, right now, she was again making a genuine effort to relate the story to him, the real story, although it was yet a very unsuccessful attempt.

"What do I hear now? Are you again going to tell me that you have something to say, but you won't say it? You can visit me tomorrow, but I don't want to know your *secret*."

He spoke in his toughest tone, silencing her once again, without letting her reveal the truth. She was disappointed. It wasn't her expectation, although it was continuously happening. She wanted to see him, to tell him the real happening of *Pour Une Nuit D'Amour*. But how unfortunate! He wasn't letting her. She felt like blurting out the story at once, but instead, he ended up blurting out his own words.

"Okay, now you're silent. I'm going for rehearsals. You can visit me or treasure your *secret* in your own cupboard."

Well, they were in two different avenues, concentrating on two different facts. She walked up to her mirror to find her worried face, changed from its bloom. She thought her worry was one, in vain. The best thing was to understand him, and that was what he needed. Yes, he needed understanding, nothing else, and she had it in plenty. What he needed she had, and she was going to let go of it at his need and request. Also, he had to be stopped from working on the wrong plot. But there was no way that she could reveal it to him.

The next minute she was ready with the bundle of papers. She met the historical marvel just once before she left when he was ready to flee. He was about to leave the beautiful seamstress disheartened; she had fallen asleep while waiting for him, knowing well that he wouldn't visit her that night.

Back in the present, the young writer took the bundle of papers with her heart full of nothing and everything.

He who is lonesome in the crowd sees thee,
Indeed, sees thee and thy lonely self,
Unable to fathom the affection which yields,
Drowns himself in the blissful sea.

She ended up concocting a brilliant idea. Perhaps, she could write to him what she could never speak out to him, about what really happened that night with Julien, Colombel, and beautiful Thérèse. Perhaps she could leave it there at the entrance to his apartment building, and it would go to him with the rest of his mail. So, in a while, without losing a moment, she began her letter:

I decided to write to you because there's something I need to explain about your first direction. Whenever I began to say it to you, you reacted at the very first word I spoke, and my attempt was futile, so here I write… Did you really think that Pour Une Nuit D'Amour ended like that? No, it didn't. Even the creator of the characters was in a dilemma about it. Thérèse never took advantage of Julien's innocence or his one-sided love. It ended up differently. I don't want you to fail in your plot. Let me explain it to you.
It's something very important that I need to tell you.

She ended her letter there, being very straightforward, not wanting to mention anything else; she included no address, no salutation. Her letter was a challenging one, but it didn't express her struggle to shield him from all inconveniences and dangers, which was the other fact that she wanted to disclose to him: her identity. The best method of delivering the letter was, just as she had already decided, leaving it in the lobby with the rest of his mail, and that was what she did the following day on her way to the campus. She knew that things had to be done systematically, being well aware that there were men who followed her. But this time it wasn't the easiest. The scrutiny she did on the road wasn't very useful.

There were men following her, according to the instructions given to them. They watched her get into a trishaw which stopped at an apartment building. She handed over an envelope to the security guard there. Next, she headed to the campus. The men weren't instructed to do more than spying on her whereabouts, so they turned back to pass the gathered facts to their leading source.

She, fully unaware of what was happening around her, attended her morning lectures. She was happy that she wrote him a letter. He would read it, and finally, he would let her express herself. Yes, at last, he would end his delusion about *Pour Une Nuit D'Amour*, the large misconception he was tremendously confident about. She was in a blissful slumber about everything that was happening around her. She went home at the end of her session. It was late, and she was happy to be home before it was dark, in the twilight. She entered thinking of embracing some rest, after a long day, but the obvious trouble awaited her. Someone else had entered her home way before her.

She dreaded his sight, the man who was sitting in the armchair sipping a beverage from her own mug.

"You have an excellent taste. This is the best coffee I've ever tasted. And having it in your own mug is wonderful," he said, taking a sip.

She turned back to run away, but some strong hands stopped her, and she was weakened by the understanding that he wasn't alone there. He was the chief, and he was always accompanied by his subordinates. They brought her to him and made her stand in front of their chief.

"Why are you so scared? I'm not going to harm you."

She became feeble by the hands that continued to grasp her tight from either side. Frightened and unable to keep up with their hold on her, she almost fainted, but the two men made sure that she didn't fall down.

"So, I hear that you were out this morning, visiting someone in town, delivering a letter. What were you carrying in that envelope? May I know?"

He walked up to her, leaving the mug on the coffee table and stopped right in front of her eyes. He found pleasure in the position, but she was facing utter unpleasantness, so she turned her face away in a quick motion. He gave out an insulting laugh, a quick one, and slowly turned her face back to him with his rough hand. She was nothing but a trapped bird with no hope of escape. The two men, holding her from either side, were gradually becoming more difficult. He smiled the most sardonic smile, and slowly turned his smile into laughter, blurting out his words.

"Looks like the little bird has no strength to chirp. Things would have been much easier if you listened and came home without roaming around in town, after school."

She feared his words and dreaded facing him, so she slowly turned her face down, making him laugh louder this time.

"That's how you should be. Look down and listen when I speak to you! Even my friends are helping you. They're very kind to you. They're helping you to stand straight without falling down."

There was a pause, quite a long one before he spoke again, and she kept listening to her pounding heart trying to figure out what the next moment would be.

"Make sure, no more outings again! If you want to go, it should be with my men! I've warned you enough. Let there be no more!"

He walked to the door, indicating to the two men to follow him. She was released with a thrust, and she fell on the sofa, giving her full weight to it. With one last look at her, he disappeared behind the door with the two men. She found herself almost in a coma. It was a blackout, and she could hardly see anything around her. She became dizzy and ended up falling off the sofa, having no sense of anything around her.

Late at night, she woke up and quickly rose to her feet, recalling all the events of the day. The memory of her visitors brought her nothing but fear. She was terrified. Was she going to let him know, the professor, about her misery at this end? How would he react? Would he understand her and sympathize with her? Or would he be indifferent to it? How could he cooperate with her negativities when he was often held up with his own? Also, she was a simple, ordinary girl who lived in obscurity, not knowing that he often wondered what her strongly felt invisibility could be. Of course, she was a shadow to him, that he could never understand, but tried his best to understand.

She ended up on the balcony again, counting the planets up there and comparing herself with them; meanwhile, he was opening her letter. He smiled as he identified her handwriting, and before he read anything else, his eyes aimed at the last line.

It's something very important that I need to tell you.

Suddenly the telephone rang, and he rushed to answer it. At this time, the boy was cleaning, and he entered his master's bedroom. It took awhile to gather the dirt, wipe and vacuum. When he was leaving, the master returned to his room, after the phone call. He sat down to read the letter and realized that it wasn't there. It didn't take long for him to understand that the boy had disposed of it when he was cleaning the room, but he could still remember the last line.

It's something very important that I need to tell you.

Recalling it, he ended up coming to a misunderstanding, just like he always did. What could it be? She often spoke about it but never revealed it. How could he make her say it? She was a mysterious one with lots of concealments. But why? Why was she not divulging things to him? He could never find answers to the questions that rose in him. He never thought, even for a moment, that she held a false belief. How unfortunate! Both were lost in their false theories, each having one's own blooming reasons which were finely created.

He arrived at a decision, however, to show her indifference whenever she spoke about her *secret*, which he could never fathom, while she, on the other hand, thought that he didn't have to be told about anything because he was showing indifference. The major misunderstanding was that he never knew that she was going to tell him the truth about his first direction: the story of one night's love.

The next day, at the campus, during her break, it was a celebration. Students left the lecture hall, and she found herself in splendid isolation. She was in a slumber, dreaming about nonexistence, happy that she was finally going to inform him. The story was finally going to take the right direction. Eager to reveal it, at last, she visited him. It so happened when he was relaxing at home. She rang the doorbell.

"Did you read my letter?" she asked, as soon as she entered.

"Yes," he said, paying less attention.

"So, you don't want to know?" she asked.

"Know what?"

She was confused by his question, and he spoke again.

"So, what about it? You wrote a letter. I read it. There's nothing more about it."

She was disappointed by his reply. It looked like he was indifferent to the subject. But, really speaking, the letter was a sweet little attack on him and his dominant self, although he knew nothing about its content. She didn't know that he had failed to read the letter, except for the last line. And that was sufficient enough for the simple, ordinary girl to make a sweet attack on his gigantic self-esteem. But she could feel nothing but his indifference towards it. How unfortunate! She could never divert him from his failing; he was obstinate in his fallacy.

"So, you don't want to know about it?"

"Which?" the highly esteemed professor asked, keeping to himself his curiosity about knowing what her *secret* was, the *secret* of a simple, ordinary girl.

"I told you in my letter that I had something very important to tell you," she said.

He was silent, and in a while, she spoke again.

"You don't even know what it is," she said, disappointed.

"I don't know, and I don't want to know about it, either," he replied calmly.

She was more disappointed by his words and regretted her own effort to highlight the truth to him. Straightforward, she was one excellent insignificance. He didn't even want to know what her yearning was. The twosome didn't realize that they kept referring to two different facts, headstrong in two different avenues. However, they parted with another confirmation of their next rendezvous, which didn't appear to have any connection to a historical figure or occurrence. She was obsessed by his invitations, although she could reveal nothing to him. Her obsession was what she was eager about. In the presence of his invitations, her fear of being spied upon was absent. No force could withdraw her from her fondness, affection, and love.

She returned home, her heart full, with no consideration given to the indifference he showed. What mattered to her was that he welcomed her, with all the importance hidden under some sweet unimportance on the surface.

Finding herself isolated at home, she became fascinated by her dreaminess. The balcony was her favourite spot, where she watched the stars which confirmed her triviality. She absolutely had nothing to carry with her, no work to complete. But she was journeying through history for her own interest: to meet that great novelist, Émile Zola, and the beautiful dressmaker, Jeanne Rozerot.

19TH–20TH CENTURY

The Dreyfus Affair was still up and about, covering the nation in shields of uncertainty, for no one really knew what would happen to him. The dominant figure in political liberty, Zola, who fought to prove the innocence of Alfred Dreyfus, had fled the country after his controversial publication, *J'Accuse…!* It wasn't clear which direction things would turn.

Jeanne, the unnoticeable significance, was in the dark about the political unrest in detail, but she wanted to investigate it only for the role played in it, by the monsieur. She made sure that she was alerted about every change that took place. She began to read newspapers more than she had ever done, just to find out when he would return. At the same time, she longed for his letters. And of course, he did write to her! How amazing! Letters exchanged both ways in plenty!

At one point, she was happy when the media released the latest news about the Dreyfus Affair. The article written by the monsieur had made a significant impact on the proclamation of the release of Alfred Dreyfus. But it didn't look like it was going to happen very soon. Anyway, what made her happy was the situation of the present government. It might have been bad news to a majority or to a minority. Jeanne had no consideration of it. The government began to fall, and Jeanne had the faintest thought that the monsieur would return. And he did.

His *other wife*, dear Jeanne, was delighted about Zola's return and she waited with her heart full. Alexandrine, on the other hand, knew that he would return soon. She too waited, less enthusiastically than Jeanne anyway.

And so, he did return to both of them.

Alexandrine welcomed him with a warm, kind heart. She never wanted to part with him, nor did he want to part with her. For Jeanne, he was the past, present, and future; she could think of nothing else in his absence.

The monsieur was living his life between them, and so time passed quickly and slowly.

Jeanne waited for him in her little home. It was home for him, and she never considered it to be his second home. Really, for her, it was his only home, just like Alexandrine's was for her. Some days the monsieur woke up with Jeanne and some days, with Alexandrine.

One day, when he was at his favourite pastime, he met Thérèse de Marsanne. It was another brilliant meeting after the sudden one when she was on her balcony.

He was riding his bicycle, past an impressive, significant lake, and Thérèse was seated on its bank! The lovely didn't have the same stunning smile on her face. She sat there, looking like the contradiction of the highly dominating female that she was known as. Her eyes were focused far away as if she was trying to find something on the other side of the lake, and from time to time they were diving in the water. It wasn't clear where her eagerness was, in the water, or far away in the woods on the other side.

The monsieur went closer to her, but he was hardly noticed. Thérèse was in a world of her own. Being overwhelmed by her own striking awareness or ignorance, she was far from the lovely, happy maiden formed in everyone's eyes. Her repentant eyes definitely took the monsieur by surprise. He began to look down upon himself. Had he been wrongly informed about her? How could he be so blind? Or was he taken over by some hallucination?

He slowly walked closer and stood right next to her. Yet, there was no way of waking her up from her trance. She hardly even blinked her eyes. He had no fear of being seen by her now. He was sure that she wasn't the girl he had thought she was, and he had just been diving in his own little misunderstanding. He wanted to speak to her and tried it many times, constantly failing. Hesitant, he tried again, one last time, and at the end of it, he made up his mind to leave. He turned his head, but before he could take a single step, the so-called haughty woman woke her voice.

"Monsieur!"

He was alarmed to hear her, of course, for the first time in his life, but at the very first address, he realized that he yearned for it, as he was subtly happy about being called by her. However, she couldn't stop him. He took one step forward, perhaps with the expectation of listening to the pretty address again. Thérèse was disappointed by his reaction. She expected him to stop and come back to her, but that wasn't happening. So, she called again, and this time, it was a soft cry.

"Monsieur!"

And he stopped.

She stood up and became equal to him, although it wasn't very easy. The monsieur was, of course, thunderstruck. Pretty Thérèse, his own creation, was right in front of his eyes. He was completely stunned, beginning to understand how wrong he had been in his implicit making.

"Monsieur," she said again, this time in very soft words.

He was still silent, unable to utter a word. Two icy cold teardrops came down her cheeks, making him thoroughly regret his own invention.

"How could you do this to me, monsieur?"

He remained silent, and she spoke again.

"Your silence doesn't do anything about the injustice that's come upon me. It won't be fixed."

Thérèse was agonized, but it didn't break the silence of the other.

"You've made the whole world think that I took advantage of Julien's innocence. But I didn't. I wish I had told you before you discovered me," she explained.

"Tell me now!" he briefly said.

"I loved Colombel. I fell in love with him, and it was only him, always."

Thérèse spoke in the same disturbing voice. From time to time, her voice broke, and the monsieur listened with the sole intention of identifying.

"I agree, I didn't have that same pure intention at first, but I just couldn't help falling in love with him."

Zola was fully concentrated on her story which was easy to understand, although it was hard on him. And Thérèse continued.

"That night, he came to meet me, full of anger. He hadn't enjoyed me listening to Julien's flute. He had indirectly told me about it and was in a false belief that I was deceiving him together with Julien."

Zola became concerned, listening to the right explanation, wondering how far he had gone wrong when releasing his great work. He felt horrible, and never would he trust his instincts again.

"We ended up in a severe argument, and he was gradually becoming more and more aggressive. He wanted to have Julien killed, and I tried my best to stop him."

He listened, even more, alarmed, as the story went on.

It took a striking effect:

Julien was playing his old instrument, the flute. It was producing the most harmonious music for Thérèse. She could never turn back from it. She rested her hands on the wooden barrier of the balcony and listened to it, the most beautiful melody in the world. It was dark out there, and Julien could see the fabulous figure, although the stunning dimples in her face weren't vivid, for darkness was excessively triumphant. He was looking straight at the prettiness on the balcony, no matter how unclear her face was. The golden locks were, nevertheless, shining in the moonlight and he adored them. He enjoyed the rhythmical swinging of her head and wished that he could be closer to her.

She kissed her hand and sent it flying to him, and he, bewildered like always, kept his hand against his chest as if to ask if she sent it to him. The beauty was encouraged by his reaction and became more energetic in the process. There was no end to the kisses she was throwing in the air and he, engrossed in the beautiful incidence, was unknowingly making a heavenly tune that he had never made before.

It went on like that for quite a long time, until a figure appeared behind her who was most expected but least welcomed: young Colombel. Julien was worried. The two lovers met each other, and soon they were in each other's arms.

Julien was still playing the flute, but he was utterly distressed. The young lovers up there were embracing each other, from time to time laughing aloud at him. The innocent man, making the divine tune, was sad. Just a little while ago, beautiful Thérèse was sending him kisses flying in the air. She was exposing her affection, or he thought she was. But now, at the arrival of Colombel, things had just switched to a paradox. Julien began to grieve upon it. He didn't stop playing his flute. The melody was gradually turning into melancholia. He was weeping inside, not knowing that he was dwelling in his own exaggeration.

In truth, Colombel arrived when the beautiful blonde was in her own lovely obsession with the tune. The rhythmical movement of her head went hand in hand with the melody of the wind, making a concord, coming together with the flute.

And that was when Colombel lost it.

He took the young woman by her shoulders and shook her until she broke her lovely connection with the flute. It was a bad scene, a very bad one. She cried out loud, and so did he. The turmoil went on for some more time until they dragged themselves inside. When they were in the climax of their clash, Julien could only assume that they were making love, so he was burning inside.

In a while, he was shattered by the sound of his door which broke, and he quickly rose from his bed to meet Colombel face to face, with Thérèse behind him. She was in an unsuccessful attempt to stop her lover from doing any harm to the innocent man. After the face-to-face fight between the two men, Julien somehow managed to escape and run away. It didn't stop Colombel's hunt. He chased Julien until he managed to catch up with him at the lake, where their clash began again at an extreme level.

They didn't know that they were getting closer to the edge of the lake. They were high above it. Thérèse's efforts didn't help, as the two men were engrossed in a big fight.

What a tragedy! It happened in a flash. They fell into the water, making a splash, and young Thérèse de Marsanne became still. She ran to the edge to see the circular movement of water where they fell. It was like a whirlpool, and Thérèse kept watching. The two men came up, relieving themselves from the dive, but didn't look like they had ended their fight. They were still in each other's grasp. In a momentary flash of time, they both took a quick look at Thérèse, before they went down. And never did they come up again.

Zola was still listening, even though the story had ended. He thought there was more, and Thérèse made her pleading address again.

"Monsieur, that's my story. And that's how it ended. This is where they drowned. I've been coming here every night, ever since."

He still stood there, astonished, wondering where he went wrong. Was it a mistake? Could it be rectified? And does it have to be?

"And I never married, monsieur, although you assumed I did. I've been alone, living with the dead."

He became rapt in his own misconception. How long would his misunderstanding have its wondrous effect? Perhaps a century later, on a gigantic figure in the performing arts and an ordinary girl, a writer to whom Zola had already communicated the truth about the amazing triangle. True, she was unsuccessful in communicating it to the professor, who was living a delusive life, embracing and worshipping his own misconception, the headstrong fallacy.

It was, indeed, the supreme wisdom of the incomparable, everywhere and all around.

21st Century

She was still contemplating Julien, Colombel, and Thérèse, giving most of her attention to Julien, as his role was associated with the professor's emphasis on the solitary man who lived in the past. The professor wonderfully and unknowingly went ahead with drawing comparisons between himself and the creator of the three characters: Émile Zola.

Also, she was filling in the missing lines.
Thy indifference to the lass who ironed,
Destiny of the one who writes,
Oh, Monsieur Zola, it's a century and six!
The ample bit thou hath for me!

It was the late night, and she decided to go out to the balcony to look at the stars again to convince herself. Some stars were even speaking to her, trying their best to prove her right. Yes, they were massive planets in the sky, and she was simply a trivial being.

The breeze was lovely and gave way to her beautiful rays of thought, so she began to line up the art waves of her heart, together with a tender heart from the long-ago past: Jeanne, the seamstress.

Monsieur Zola and Thee

Controversial French novelist,
Major figure in political liberty,
Proponent of Naturalism,
I ink my pen to write thyself.

Monsieur Zola thy lonely self,
I witness after those silent years.
So broke, relied on sparrows on a sill,
Thy lonely self vigorously shines.

He who is lonesome in the crowd sees thee,
Indeed, sees thee and thy lonely self,
Unable to fathom the affection which yields,
Drowns himself in the blissful sea.

Thy indifference to the lass who ironed,
The destiny of the one who writes,
Oh, Monsieur Zola, it's a century and six!
The ample bit thou hath for me!

She picked up the phone at a moment of uncertainty, not really knowing how she was going to say it. She had to reveal the misconception he dealt in, somehow. It was his arrogant walk in the wrong direction.

"Sir, I want to see you soon," she said.

This time, he considered her tone as he realized that she was troubled. She was always full of cheer and never sounded this disturbed before. She never sounded uneasy, even during his highest levels of unease. Quite unknowingly, he was attached to her tranquility; she was tranquil when he was anything but tranquil. Most specifically, she endured his nonendurance and accepted his nonacceptance. And now, the simple, ordinary girl who was *mysterious*, in his own words, was finally going to reveal the truth about her, her *secret*, or he thought she was.

"Yes," he said.

"But there's something I want to ask you before I come. Please don't misunderstand me when I ask you this; really, I don't mind even if you think poorly of me for this…"

She was endlessly repeating herself, and he became impatient, but remained silent, giving her time to speak.

"Sir, please make sure that there's no one home when I come. Make sure you send that boy somewhere far 'cause I have something to tell you, you alone, and it's very important."

He stopped at her words. This was very strange, a bizarre turn from where he thought it might go when she started. Throughout, he had been inviting her home, but now it was her idea, and she sounded even more *mysterious* this time.

"Well, then, tomorrow will be the ideal day. I'm home the whole day. You can come in the morning."

"Seven thirty is the time I come for lectures, sir. I'll come to you before I go there."

"That's excellent."

The conversation ended there. She went back inside and found herself in the kitchen with a glass of icy cold water. After placing the water jug back in the refrigerator, she came back to see a tiny eye-fly in the glass, in a life struggle. She made the insect climb on her finger, and the little life was happy. It crawled along her hand and flew away, making its redeemer even happier. She took another glass of water and drank it in one brief guzzle, then another and another. By the third one, she felt that it was enough.

She had just one more day to meet the professor. She was determined that she was going to expose the right story, this time. Also, she summoned the courage to reveal the truth about her identity, although it was a challenging task. He always understood her as simple obscurity. She had something that she kept hidden from him. He was trying his best to come to his own understanding about it, but he couldn't. When she didn't reveal herself, he decided to show his indifference to it, as it was an attack on his self-esteem and dominance. However, at last, she decided to give in.

But how?

How was she going to tell him that a few years ago, she had been married to his opponent in politics? How was she going to tell him that she kept it hidden from him throughout? How would he take it when he heard that she was held distraught by this man? Knowing that he was in political contention with her former husband, she still visited him? She fell in love with him? She encouraged him to invite her to his home, knowing very well that he was completely in the dark about her identity? How would he look at it? Wouldn't he appreciate it? Or would he?

She had less sleep that night, switching herself between the balcony and her little bed, covered with the blanket. The flowery blanket, dim as ever, was giving her enough comfort. However, she did nothing but move from bed to balcony and balcony to bed.

Close to midnight, she heard the same terrifying hit on her door that she always dreaded. It was the only visitor that could ever be. Yes, it was him, and she waited without moving, wrapped in the blanket as tight as she could. It was a thunderstorm outside and looked like she wasn't the least bit affected by it, despite her fear; she had just passed the thin line between fear and neglect. So, she waited. But the next moment, one of her visitors entered through the balcony and opened the door for the main visitor, who entered with the most wicked smile on earth. He was surprised, however, to see the girl very calm, sitting on the couch, not bothered in the least. He didn't enjoy her silence, so he raised his voice.

"So, the beauty looks like she doesn't care anymore. How did you get that strength, may I ask?"

She was still silent, locking herself much tighter in the blanket. Being seated at the very end of the couch, she was indirectly leaving space for him, and he made use of it.

"I'm asking you a question," he said firmly as he moved towards her and sat right next to her.

She looked like she was far away, not really aware that he was close to her, or even that someone was sitting there trying to drag her attention. He gave her some more time, but circumstances were the same, and he lost it. He pulled her head towards him, and she couldn't ignore it.

"Won't you answer me? I am right here. Speak up!"

This time she began to rise, or rather, fall down on the floor, and a very tolerant cry came out of her, which reached as far as the soft breeze outside and disappeared into it.

"Can you see me?" he asked.

"Yes," she murmured, nodding her head to support her reply.

He gave out a loud laugh. Helpless, she tried to relieve herself from his grip, but it was a clear failure.

"I've seen you very uneasy these days, busy as ever, so many outings?" he said, or rather, asked in a questioning tone.

"Yes," she timidly replied.

"May I know any reason for that?"

"I just had some banking to do and also some shopping for clothes."

"I see. But your outings have become more frequent, and it makes me think that something's up to no good. Remember, next month it's the elections."

The two men stood there at the door guarding the torture, giving maximum support to their chief. She was struggling to escape, even if it was just a dream now. She had no hope of it.

"I'm just doing my day-to-day work," she whispered.

Again, the same evil smile appeared on his face. It gradually turned into laughter, and enjoying his grip, he rose to his feet, making her follow him.

She stood up most hesitantly, feeling weak, trying to keep herself together.

"Something tells me that you're up to no good. Just be careful! Let me not catch you riding a galloping horse! If I do, you'll be in big trouble."

His words were menacing, and they fit well in her ears. Without warning, he drew her close to smell her fragrance before he got rid of her aggressively, just like he always did. She was tossed away from him and thrown on the ground, and her midriff scraped on the edge of the wooden coffee table, resulting in severe pain. She felt as if a joint was dislocated somewhere around her waist.

The three men left her like that. She tried her best to stand up, but it wasn't easy to do. She felt as if her body was broken into two parts at her waist. With difficulty, she rose to her feet and stayed there until she felt healed. And eventually, she did.

A sudden decision was made, and she knew that it was the right one. She had to leave her present dwelling and hide somewhere that they would not be able to find her. That was her only escape. Yes, she was going to do it. It had to happen in secret, but soon. No one had to know it, as it might result in danger—it might reach the antagonistic source.

She stood up, giving her weight to the coffee table and realized that she could hardly walk, but somehow, she managed to get herself to her bed. Her mind ran to the professor, who was also busy with his political campaign. He was a shadow, a clear shadow, just like she was to him. He didn't have to know about her connection to his dogmatic political rivals. But why not? Well, he would be muddled by the very fact, and that was the last thing she wanted. She had to be the redeemer of his aches and by no means did she want to make them worse, so she confirmed her own decision to endure everything by herself, to face the agony and shield him.

She called him again, although she didn't really know why.

"So, is it confirmed? Are we meeting tomorrow morning?" she asked.

Her call surprised him just like her request to meet him. She definitely had something essential to convey to him.

"Now, how many times did I tell you? Please come!" he said.

His tone was friendly and endearing; it made her laugh for a quick moment, a very brief laugh, forgetting about her wounded waist. She made the best of it and laughed, making him believe that nothing else was going on, except a lighthearted, joyous conversation.

"I'm scared now. I don't know what you're going to do tomorrow," he said in a very joyful tone, making her laugh even more.

"Oh, don't be scared of me! Please don't!" she replied, laughing, ready for the wonderful day, the day of disclosure of many secrets.

19th–20th Century

Zola found himself with Jeanne soon after meeting Thérèse. His heart was heavy for the deception he had dealt in, throughout the years, from the day he created his unmatchable story, *Pour Une Nuit D'Amour*. He met Jeanne, but it didn't look like things were very normal between them.

"Why are you looking worried, monsieur?" she asked.

"I'm fine," he replied.

Her heart wept as she saw the grief in his eyes. But he looked like he preferred to be left alone; she didn't want to intervene, nor did she want him to be left alone.

He went to the patio and felt the breeze outside, and she followed him. They were both outside on the patio for quite some time, Jeanne counting stars and the monsieur repenting over Colombel, Julien and mostly Thérèse. Suddenly, there appeared the future pair: the professor, still blissfully drowning in the same misconception and the girl who wrote, who was still trying to rescue him from the drowning. Yes, they appeared before the eyes of the beautiful mademoiselle and the monsieur. It was an amazing meeting.

Zola tried but failed to communicate to the professor, who understood nothing as he couldn't withdraw himself from his self-possessed drowning. The efforts made by his writer to convey the truth to him had ended up in a failure. Zola and the professor were both very similar, except for the amount of self-esteem each possessed. Zola readily withdrew himself from his misconception, but the professor made no such withdrawal. He always dealt with the same fallacy, not only when releasing his first direction, but even otherwise.

Jeanne looked at the modern-day writer and gave her a smile, making her well-equipped.

21st Century

The next day was another bright day. She had forgotten about the previous night. It was only his lovely invitation, which was encouraged by her own, that mattered. Yes, she had invited him to invite her, making it a mutual invitation.

What would she wear? She took out a silky frock designed in white and bright blue. It was the ideal one. She dressed herself in it and went up to the mirror to see her face. It glowed in love, more than any other day. She tied her hair into a braid, making sure that it was neatly combed. In her blameless, very simple, but complicated state of being in love, she totally forgot all the unpleasantness that existed around her. She was simply ready.

She didn't even know how she made her way there, but before she could think of anything else but him, she was there in front of his door, passing the distance between them: the lobby, the elevator and everything else. And he opened the door. They looked at each other and smiled. She walked in and locked the door behind, listening to his appealing words.

"I sent the boy out, and he won't be back till tomorrow."

She smiled again, and he immediately withdrew himself to answer the ringing telephone. Her eyes moved around and ended up resting on the photographs. She went through them until he returned, admiring the pleasant smiles in the portrait she loved.

"So now tell me! What do you have to tell me?" he softly asked, walking towards her.

He stopped right next to the window, facing her. She could see outside, through the window, but there were no seagulls; he wouldn't have seen them, even if there had been any, as he had all his senses on her. He couldn't withdraw himself from her, but he didn't realize that she had her eyes on the smiles in her favourite picture. Looking at his forlorn self together with the face full of smiles in the portrait, and recalling the visitors of the night before, she ended up falling into the same liveliness, bearing up to the agony around her waist.

"So, I never said I'm going to say it, sir," she said in her usual playful tone, hiding all her agonies behind her cheer.

She continued her talkativeness, looking at him, and he stayed silent, smiling.

"Oh, how interesting! Earlier I was the scared one, and now it's you! This is so interesting. I never thought that I was so scary. Have I really frightened you a lot?"

She was almost singing her words, and he stayed listening to her with the same smile, admiring her song. Oh, what a bright, happy little charm! What liveliness he saw right in front of his eyes! But really, what enormous endurance he didn't see behind that smile!

At one strikingly felt, unexpected moment, he broke his silence and walked towards her, abruptly halting her rhythm, and she was stunned. He embraced her, reaching her trembling lips as softly as he could. His hands were obstinate on the wound around her waist. It hurt her, but she ignored it. She was wonderfully charmed in his arms.

"I won't let you leave today … won't let you leave…," he said, repeating in a murmur.

"I can be your friend, at your hard times, sir. I want to be so…to be with you at difficult times," she whispered, giving up herself to him.

He was soothed by her understanding self, and he welcomed her deep inside his heart. His hands were gentle, and she felt that she was the most delicate woman on earth. Now it looked like he was the guest and she, the host. Indeed, they were taking turns between guest and host. And he came to a sudden interval. She, in a dazzle, showed no interest in finding out any reason for his pause. She didn't have to wait long for it, anyway.

"Come!" he said, holding her hand and walking to the interior of his home.

She followed him, and he was charmed. It was a long walk. They both sat down on his bed, and he began to feel the tenderness of her hair. He was just beginning to believe in them, and she, indeed, let him, treasuring him in her heart. He reached her lips, making it endless. But at one point she stopped.

She smiled with her understanding self, and he embraced her smile deep within.

He became thoughtful for a moment, and she understood him much better. That was what he needed. He was building his dwelling in her, and she in him, although he was in total darkness about her inner episodes and, of course, she too about his.

A few more hours joined the past, with the harmonious pair resting in each other's depth.

Now she was never going to mention her identity. She lacked neither the strength nor the courage for that. How alarmed he would be, to hear the truth about her! She dreaded him knowing about it, so she was determined not to disclose it. It was impossible to make up her mind to say it, and the truth about *Pour Une Nuit D'Amour* was nowhere there now, anyway.

"Tell me what you want to say, at least now!" he whispered.

"Maybe I'll write to you," she said in a much softer voice.

Her frequent smile and playful tone misled him. He didn't realize that she was at a dead end.

She turned to him in a flash.

"Can I send my letter with a friend?"

"Yes."

"Will you read it?"

"Yes."

There was silence again. She was the girl who spent time among stars, comparing the immensity of the universe with her triviality. However, now things had changed, so he didn't stop to ask her more questions or to understand her. There was a simple, alluring girl right next to him, and he was enchanted. That was all that mattered. He didn't waste time finding out why she made an incomprehensible visit to him, all of a sudden. What mattered now was that she was there with him.

The pair came back to themselves at the ring of the telephone. They both rose to their feet. She walked to the adjoining washroom.

"There's a green towel there. You can use it," he said before he picked up the receiver.

She stood in front of the wash basin and took a deeper look at her face in the mirror before soaking her face with water. Her eyes with their little pupils were very clear. She admired them, as much as they admired her.

She stood still, looking at her reflection for a while. And yes, there was the green towel, and she took it to her hand.

Coming out, she realized that he was still on the phone call. She entered the room again. Seeing her, he placed his finger across his mouth as if to ask her to be silent. So, she walked out again, thinking of taking a walk in his home. And she did, a brief one, looking at the pictures, returning the same smiles to the portrait, finding the leftovers of the herbal porridge from that morning, in the kitchen. She stopped for a while at the window, in an attempt to find a seagull and quickly returned to him, listening to his very expressive words.

"Where is this girl now?"

And she appeared before his eyes.

"Come! Stay with me here!" he said, resting in bed, his head turned towards the ceiling.

She reached up to him, reposed her head on his shoulder, turning away, and he began to admire her hair again. The lovely duo was very much in harmony. He smiled, pleased with her vivacity. She suddenly remembered the night before and became engrossed in agony again, but in a quick second, she switched her emotion, turning to be as happy as she could. He didn't have to be disturbed with her griefs; she was the giver, not the recipient.

She made a sharp turn towards him, hurting her waist, and he noticed that she was in pain.

"What happened?" he asked.

"It just hurts. Something's wrong here around my waist," she said, touching and soothing her waist with her hand.

He was worried, thinking that she had got hurt in his home. She knew it, so she wished to clear his doubts.

"Did you hurt yourself? How did it happen?"

"I don't know, sir. Just hurts. Something happened to my waist yesterday when I got up from bed. I think I was in an awkward position."

"Oh, it was already there when you came. You must take treatment."

She nodded her head, giving him a pleasant smile, hiding her wound and all her other wounds behind. In a flash, she turned herself all the way to him in an attempt to tell her tale. No matter how successful her effort was, she could only repeat her question.

"Will you read my letter?"

"Yes," he said again.

"Won't blame me for not telling you all this time?"

"No."

There was silence again for some time until they both realized that they had to part, he with nothing but thoughts of seeing her again soon and she with doubts that perhaps they might never see each other again when he got to know her true identity.

She rose to her feet and started brushing her hair, and he watched her. She whispered the difference. "Straightened my hair."

"Beautiful," he murmured, pleased.

He stood up from the bed while she rested her eyes on a significant object, and she was stunned. It was an electric iron on an ironing board and his chemise ready to be ironed. She heard a sweet voice from history, and she turned to him with a heavy heart concealed with a smile.

"Who irons your clothes, sir?"

"The boy."

He gave a quick reply and walked to the kitchen, and she made use of the time left for herself. She plugged in the iron, and it warmed up. A delicate voice from the past was calling her. She was relaxed. She felt as if she was travelling in the opposite direction with time. Her hand, gently held by a century old tenderness, softly moved with the tool on his chemise. It was done soon, and she kept it on the board. Excellent!

The professor came back and walked towards her. He had her in his arms again, reaching her lips and feeling her tenderness. She was softened. It took a long time.

They both walked to the door, and she repeated her obvious question.

"So, you won't blame me when you read my letter?"

"No," he most politely said, turning her face towards him and feeling the softness of her forehead with his lips. "And I don't like when you keep saying it and asking me repeatedly."

She made a modest movement with her head, promising him nothing but modesty. It was a heavenly contact, and he was attached to it. She opened the door and looked outside to see if anyone could see them.

"Is anyone watching?" he asked, as he was standing inside and couldn't see what happened outside.

"No," she whispered.

She closed the door for a quick second and planted her soft lips gently on his forehead, and he gave her the most endearing smile. Again, they fell into each other's arms, unable to part. It took a long time, and the door opened again. They parted. He watched her walk into the elevator. While the door closed, they looked at each other and smiled.

Leaving him in the dark, she came down, carrying the heaviest heart. She went back home, having her thoughts on the following day and her secret getaway. Every little moment thereafter was spent cautiously in gloom, the longest moments in the world.

It was the longest night. There was a mutual agreement between herself and any kind of blissful slumber—they were far from each other. That was their only intimacy. She was walking back and forth between the balcony and her bed as there was nowhere else she could go. The sky was dull, and she could find no bright planets in it, even to measure their immensities, emphasizing on her own triviality. At one moment she turned towards her bed, quickly turning off the light for the flying insects to fall down. Some of them fell down dead, and some were still alive, making her realize that she couldn't save them all. However, it wasn't clear if she was convinced of anything. She felt weak. Coming back to the balcony, she picked up the phone and made her call in a moment of panic, and the professor answered. He was happy to receive a call from her, not knowing that he was just going to receive the most unexpected news.

"Sir," she began. "I thought I'd say it now, what I came to tell you."

"Okay, say it now!" He became very enthusiastic, eager to hear it from her, not knowing what drastic news he was just about to hear.

"Sir, can we meet now?"

"What? When?"

"Now."

"Okay, come now! I'll wait for you."

His expectations were evident in his tone, and she could hardly respond as she knew the severity of her identity. But she managed to express herself.

"I'll be there soon, sir."

It was the longest hour. She was going to mention the kind of fact about her that he never expected to hear. He didn't know that the most severe part was yet to come. He was lost in a world of his own, feeling for some reason, the profound loss of an ordinary girl who understood the writing of his depth and brilliantly put it, in words, on paper. He didn't know that on the surface of writing about Émile Zola, she was painstakingly writing nothing but his heart. He didn't know that she was empathizing with his sorrows. He didn't even know that in her journey into history to meet the controversial novelist, she had ended up meeting him, the professor, her dictator, the forlorn. He could feel some kind of loss that he was going to face as if it was going to be only him and his lonely home. The visitor, the girl who wrote him, his heart, his depth was going to be absent. Yes, he could thoroughly feel her now. He felt that he was going to be in some kind of a lonely hold. He gradually realized that he didn't long for her visits to travel through history, but to travel through his loneliness. How was it that he didn't understand it earlier? And why didn't he mention it to her?

One more hour was spent. She was still on the balcony trying to find a planet, and he was drawing pictures on the ceiling, pictures of a modest girl this time, the girl who wrote his depth. It was a realization that he could hardly comprehend. Suddenly, his doorbell rang, he opened the door, and she ended up in his arms.

"Tell me!"

"Sir, I was married to the leader of your opposition."

"Married? My opposition?"

"Yes, sir…"

She related her story, at last, taking her own time; it was hard for the listener. It took a long time to describe her past and present. And he managed to grasp the two salient facts which were the hardest on him. One was that she had been married to the leader of his opposition. The other was that she was continuously distraught by him. They both brought about one simple truth between the lines: She had endured him, the professor, and his dominance over her while being victimized by his own opponent. He stood still, unable to take it all at once. He started at a small-scale, with his own capacity of understanding and gradually expanded it within himself. The process took a long time, and finally, he began.

He took his first steps towards his final disappointing discovery: He had always viewed her as a simple, ordinary girl, but now, she was just beginning to be the contrary in his eyes. What disturbed him most was the untold truth he saw between the lines: She had endured him while being prey to his own rival. He slowly began to understand that measuring her level of endurance wasn't an easy task. Her capacity to endure was too much on him. He wondered how that incalculable capacity could be possible in such ordinariness, and in front of that enormous strength, the most dominant man on earth was just about to face a nervous breakdown.

"How could you hide this from me all this time?" he asked, almost in a whisper.

"Sir, I was simply…"

She began to speak but could reveal nothing.

"Go through such torture and bear it up all by yourself and not even tell me? Why are you saying it now? There's no point in saying it now!" he cried out in sorrow.

"Sir, I tried to…"

She gave another effort to speak, and it was yet again a failure.

"And why are you saying it now anyway? So late? I was thinking, always trying to figure out what it could be. Even when I was sleeping, I was trying to guess it, what it could be that you were always trying to tell me but kept postponing," he cried out intensely.

"Sir, whenever I tried to say it, you always told me that you don't even want to know it and that's why I didn't tell you," she managed to blurt out at last.

"I said I don't want to know it 'cause you weren't saying it," he said, at a rapid tone.

"Well, I didn't say it 'cause you said you don't want to know it," she said in a soft whisper.

They were in two streams, flowing in opposite directions. Meeting at equilibrium but diverting from there, they didn't come to any kind of understanding. And he spoke again.

"Now that you say that he was always following you and torturing you, how would I know if you didn't tell me? How would I know? And the elections are next month. Does he know that you've been visiting me?"

"No, sir, he doesn't know."

"Oh, how could you do this? Just remain silent about it without telling me? Being tortured throughout and hide it from me?"

His tone was stern, and she began to feel remorseful about her own imaginary fantasies. She slowly walked to the window. Looking up at the sky through his window, she wondered if she could find a star, but failed.

She blamed them, anyway, all the planets in the sky for their own triviality. And she turned to him again. He was still in the storm of realizing how wonderfully she had endured him throughout, carrying her own burden of agony on her shoulders. Oh, how excellently and silently she had concealed a marvel within her tender self without even letting him notice when he had really been thinking the opposite. She wonderfully hit the self-esteem of the most dominant man on earth. He felt as if he had been pierced with the sharpest knife in the world. The knife had been so sharp that he hadn't even felt it until some time after. He couldn't help looking down upon himself.

His anger was at the highest pitch, with the same thought haunting him. It was a thought that repeatedly came to him, attacking his self-image: How could she keep her sorrows and grievances caused by his opponent, concealed from him while enduring his dominance? He realized that he had to change the picture he had of the everyday, common girl he had known. His own understanding of this truth was the biggest attack on him, and there was only one way to relieve himself of this disgrace.

"Tell me! Did you tell me earlier that you were married to him? Did you or not? I'm asking you! Did you say it to me?"

His severity was in a constant upward struggle and tears came down her cheeks, worsening it all. Looking at her face, he remembered the tears shed by the pair of beautiful hazel eyes long ago, and ever since, he hadn't been able to stand tears in any form, so he wasn't going to tolerate them coming from the simple, modest girl who had just turned out to be a marvel. He was broken into pieces and was in an unsuccessful attempt to gather himself to face the battle with the most dominant woman on earth. He gave his sternest command.

"Stop it!"

But his words made no change in her.

"Sir, also I want to tell you that *Pour Une Nuit D'Amour* is…"

"Enough of it now. There's nothing more to talk about. You failed to tell me all about this and all of a sudden you decide to say it. Why? Why now? There's no need to say it now. Keep it all to yourself!"

"Sir, the plot in your story…"

"Enough!" he screamed.

Her face gave him no expression, but she had tears pouring down with no attempt to hold them back, and he couldn't endure it. How pathetic!

And what a contrast! He was nowhere near that enduring marvel and was about to fall into a severe psychological collapse, unable to endure her endurance. Oh, how unfortunate! She was failing now, victimized by his inner failure, being prey to his defeat.

He cried out his command again, "Stop it!"

The conversation ended there, sliding her into a terrible state of confusion. She quickly left him and flew towards her home. For a long time, she kept looking at herself in the mirror, finding a stranger with pale eyes and hollowed cheeks. She forgot everything about him and concentrated on herself. And he forgot everything about himself and concentrated on the terrible blow he received from a simple, ordinary, common girl.

She spent a sleepless night again, sitting down at the mobile lamp, turning it off and on at regular intervals, not knowing what her next move should be. She blamed herself for the confusion she had created.

He spent the night overwhelmed by an inventive thought that was formulating. Perhaps she had maintained silence, keeping him in the dark for a valid reason. Yes, perhaps she had kept her identity hidden all the time for a nefarious purpose. And what could that be? Well, she had mentioned her connection with his opposition, although that had been in the past. Well then, perhaps she had visited him because she had been still helping them. Oh, yes, she had been simply spying on him then. In one devastating situation she had failed to act her role anymore, so she had decided to run away. How wonderfully she had designed the art! Yes, she was a spy, a spy indeed, a spy who came from the opposition.

He fell into an unimaginable level of rage, unknowingly and blissfully drowning in delusion; that was a way of triumphing over her: the ordinary marvel. He was unable to fathom anything else beyond his miserable belief, he hardly ever identified. Amazing! The more he fell into that uncontrollable level of self-deception, the more she ended up sympathizing with him. She was at the extreme level of empathy, and he was at a dangerous level of self-deception. So, they most spontaneously exceeded equilibrium—he reached the highest level of rage derived from self-deception, and she reached the highest level of sympathy derived from her failure to explain. They were a wonderful duo in mutual misunderstanding, just like they were in harmony in mutual understanding, the other day.

Another night was spent, the final night, with the same fuming misconception at his end and the dangerous sympathy at her end; he was drowning in a never-ending sea of effortless self-deception, and she was turning the light off and on, trying to find a resolution, to save him from the drowning.

Soon it was morning, and she realized that she and the portable lamp had a common understanding. It was wonderful! At certain times, the light turned off and on for her without her intervention. She knew nothing about what was happening on the other side of the world. She only knew that she was going to hand over the key to the owner, as discussed and most cautiously leave her dwelling in a few hours. But she felt incomplete. Something was drawing her back, and it was him. He had to be informed, at least at the last moment, about *Pour Une Nuit D'Amour*, the first direction of the gigantic figure in the performing arts.

The phone, which was lying on the table, got hold of her again.

"Sir, can I come, just once? Let me explain it to you. Let me speak to you, just five minutes? Just want to tell you something about your plot…"

She was still making the same modest request at the dead end of her sympathy, and now it seemed like she needed sympathy, to sympathize with his unconscious psychic torment.

"No!" he cried out. "You're a liar. From the beginning you knew, you knew you were my enemy and I didn't know it. You were hiding it from me. You were simply deceiving me. You! The little deceit! You came here to spy on me, and now you're trying to approach me to put me in a big mess. Don't try to meet me again! Don't ever call me again! You're a spy, a spy! Yes, you're a spy!"

"Sir, I'm not a spy. I'm not trying to bring any trouble to you. I didn't even tell you about it 'cause I didn't want to disturb you," she explained.

"Then why are you telling me now?" he screamed.

"Because I love you," she cried out in the most quivering voice.

The whole world stopped with her words, and he felt triumphant to hear them coming from her.

"If you loved me, you should have told me who you were long ago." He paused. "And I don't want to listen to it now."

His tormented past fell in his memory again, and it was impossible to connect it with the present. Wasn't it the same dismay, torturing him again now? He withdrew himself before any collision happened in his mind. She was a spy. Yes, she was nothing but a spy. In fact, that was the only thought that he could entertain to convince himself of triumph. That was the only thought he could destroy her with. But for her, it was the hugest volcano eruption, and she fell down on the ground, struggling with the very same level of endurance. And, of course, she shouldered her newest identity that she knew nothing about: spy. It immensely differed from her real identity that she had failed to reveal to him on time.

Some more hours were spent in the same air, the same surroundings, the same misunderstanding, the misconception, and the self-deception, as well as the same dangerous sympathy. Finally, it was time for her escape. The key was handed over on time, and she got into the taxi that came to take her. It was done vigilantly, as quickly as possible, for she knew that she had regular invaders. However, this time she was fortunate. No one tracked her, and she vanished in the taxi, giving a last look at the little space that had accommodated her for years.

The taxi moved past familiar communities, buildings, trees, and people, but her heart was empty. There was absolutely nothing in it, just her voice at work, and she directed the driver to the four walls that waited for her, although the dweller was drowning. The taxi stopped there, and she got out. Being a familiar visitor, she could easily pass, and she was in front of his door sooner than she had expected. She rang the doorbell but received no response. She turned the lock; the door opened, and she slowly walked in. The sound of water made her understand that he was taking a shower, so she waited for him in the living area, receiving regular smiles from the face in the portrait.

Jeanne Rozerot, the seamstress, strengthened her with a brave smile from a century in the past. The young writer returned the smile, promising her to be of equal valour. The girl who wrote and the girl who seamed. What difference did they have? None, absolutely none, except their titles: seamstress and writer.

He was still in the same feeble debate with himself, struggling in his failure, within the same unsuccessful attempt to convince himself. He wished the water that sprang down could wash away all his failures, but it couldn't.

It took some time, and he came out, to find his frequent visitor in the living room—the girl who wrote his heart. Her sight alone made him fall into an extremely enraged psychic condition. His dangerous rage and her risky sympathy were about to clash again, face to face. He could never accept the strength of tranquility in her eyes. He feared her. In the presence of her serenity, the most dominant man on earth was just about to face his second nervous breakdown. He was never going to let her win, so he settled into a successfully unsuccessful attempt of terrorizing her.

"Out!" He walked to her, crying out in his sternest possible tone.

19TH–20TH CENTURY

"I'm leaving now," Zola said, turning to Jeanne.

"Why so early, monsieur?" she asked, in a whisper.

"It's not early. It's late now, but, never too late," he said, looking outside.

He was right; darkness was falling. He looked disappointed, and she had her eyes on him observing his face, unable to gather any reason for his distress. Thérèse de Marsanne appeared in his mind frequently, taking regular intervals between the intense life he thought he lived and his final disappointing discovery. And there stood young Jeanne Rozerot right next to him, who had first visited his house as a seamstress.

He recalled his memories of Alexandrine and also his startling discovery of Thérèse de Marsanne, the disheartened girl. He could hardly endure Jeanne, right before him. She brought colour into his lonely life, sang him songs and loved him. However, she wasn't the same eagerness now. In his failing heart at the encounter with Thérèse de Marsanne, he began to fear his meeting with Jeanne, and Jeanne alone.

"Oh, this double life, I thought would bring me happiness, has brought me to a dead end of sorrow," he muttered.

"Monsieur?" Jeanne asked, unable to hear him well.

"I'm going!" he cried out loud.

Jeanne, puzzled, walked towards him and he stepped back.

"Stop!" he screamed. "Don't come near me!"

The words entered her like thunder. Jeanne stopped there, unable to really understand him, but, of course, shouldering his change. It was a striking moment of endurance in the inconsistent, ephemeral human mind, where nothing was permanent or everlasting.

"I'm going!" he screamed in his sternest voice as he stepped out, and Jeanne watched him.

21st Century

"Out!"

He walked to her, crying out louder than earlier. She looked at him. He was looking fresh, right after a shower, wearing the same green towel around his waist, the towel he had offered to her, had shared with her, the other day. Now he was celebrating in it, the inconsistent, ephemeral human mind where nothing was permanent or everlasting, completely unaware that she was celebrating a moment of endurance in the same inconsistency, at the same time.

"Why are you here? Out! Call the police! You've entered by force? To spy? Out!" he screamed.

She was drawn back. In a moment, she was standing right next to the table, placed in the very front. But she didn't really know how she reached there. It was the same table she used to sit at, to take down dynamic dictation when he related his untold story to her. Although he was wonderfully disturbed, he was also happy about her move. He gripped her by her shoulders, and she felt uncomfortable. The most dominant man on earth was falling into a fantastic psychic drama, very different from the roles he really played as a performing artist. This time it was no role-play, no drama; it was a reality. He was in an uncontrollable level of rage in front of her remarkable strength of tranquility. The simple, ordinary girl had turned out to be a marvel, and he could never accept it. He looked into her eyes, tired and weary. They weren't giving him the same appeal. He feared them to the utmost. In front of her strong composure, he felt very small and was facing his next enormous nervous breakdown.

"Out! I'll call the police! You're a spy!" he screamed again.

He was continuously terrorizing her to pacify himself from the terror he was in. The most dominant man on earth was in a struggle, feeling that he was just nothing, in the presence of an ordinary, modest marvel. Some words came out of her in a whisper, but she didn't know what they were. She was in a failing effort to convey something to him—the truth about Julien, Colombel and Thérèse de Marsanne. He was in a gradual rise in his rage and abruptly loosened his hold, letting her go. In her favourite portrait, there were different smiles this time, and they spoke to her in a soft whisper:

Oh, my son was the same when he was little. When the formula milk was late, he cried in the same manner.

She looked at her smiles with a note of promise while listening to his words far away.

"Call the police! Out! She's a spy! A spy! Out! Now there'll be a crowd here to see what's going on! Out! Call the police!"

He was in an immensely unsteady firmness. The same condition seemed to continue for a long time. She walked through the door and into the elevator, that locked her inside and brought her down to the taxi.

19TH–20TH CENTURY

Zola reached his home, distressed and alarmed. He couldn't gather his mind together. His efforts to prove the innocence of Dreyfus hadn't been successful yet, as Dreyfus was still in jail. Thérèse troubled him for his realization of his own erroneous creation. Also, he was more disheartened by his misdeed with Alexandrine and Jeanne. He was in the misconception that the young seamstress who had brought him happiness was the reason for his muddled life now.

The following evening, he attended a social gathering with Alexandrine and returned home. He locked the window and the door, just like he did every day and went to bed without staying up too late. His mind drifted from Dreyfus, Alexandrine, and Thérèse and ended up on Jeanne, who appeared to be his prime disturbance now. He was focused on the ceiling where all memories were drawing their wonderful art.

The chimney was fixed to give enough warmth, but it wasn't working well. There was an outflow of carbon monoxide, prepared to take all of him. He was drowning in it. What a blissful drowning! He wasn't going to face any battles again. It was going to end. He saw Jeanne far away, but he made up his mind quickly, to think that she was nonexistent.

Alexandrine woke up unable to breathe through the carbon monoxide around her. She found him on the ground and called the doctors. It was too late, of course. Too late.

In a little dwelling far away, the little seamstress, Jeanne, the pure heart, was still engrossed in measuring the planets, contrasting them with her own triviality, when Alexandrine sent a note to her, letting her know about her loss. Hearing this most distressing news, she fell down on the ground and immediately rose again, concluding with herself.

21st Century

The professor was still in his excellently vibrant misconception about the wonderful writer of his depth. It was, somewhat, the same misconception he was in, about everything else in the world. He lay down in bed that night, drawing the brilliant art of the same remorseful memories. He was the actor, the dramatist and also the audience of it. He had no escape from it. However, he was happy that she was nowhere in his art. He looked deep into the ceiling trying to find her, but she wasn't there. He was thrilled that she was nonexistent. And that was precisely what he made up his mind to think. Yes, he trained his mind to believe that he never knew her, and no such writer ever visited him.

It was quite late, and the boy was worried. The master was in a dilemma, and no one could approach him. The boy knew nothing about the reason for it. The last visit of his marvellous writer and almost everything about her had been an enormous attack on his self-esteem, and it had brought down his self-control. The boy slowly walked towards him to speak to him, but he changed his mind and quickly returned to the kitchen.

The professor was still aiming at the ceiling, happy that he couldn't see his heart's writer anywhere there. He gave one more attempt to find her and was delighted that she wasn't a part of his art. He made up his mind to think that he never even met her, so when someone asked about her, he could easily say that he never knew a writer as such.

He, the gigantic figure in the performing arts, released his first direction with the same misconception about Julien, Colombel and, most of all, about Thérèse de Marsanne, no matter how hard Zola had tried to communicate the truth to him through his frequent visitor, the girl who wrote. And of course, another writer just like her, or not at all like her, came to please him, then another and another and also another. There was an endless line of writers. He was equally charmed, sometimes more and sometimes less. But none could write his depth. Yes, no one wrote his heart. Every night he was focused on the ceiling to view the same remorseful art. He was drowning in it. What a blissful sea! What a blissful drowning!

One afternoon, he was working at his table and the boy, puzzled, decided to ask him about her. He slowly approached the question just like he always did.

"Sir, why hasn't she come for a long time?"

The professor ignored his question and went on with his work, but the boy didn't give up.

"Sir, she hasn't visited for a long time," he said, this time, in an affirmation.

"Who?" the professor asked, having his eyes on his work and trying his best to exhibit indifference.

"One who came from the university? The girl who wrote?" the boy asked again.

"Which?" he indifferently confirmed and silenced the boy.

Far away, she stood in her patio with a glass of water in her hand, no longer comparing the immensity of the universe with her triviality.

Suddenly something drew her attention: a tiny ant drowning in the water in her glass. Her heart was filled with sympathy, and in a sudden flash of a moment, she placed her finger across the water and watched the little life climb on it. She was happy.

The little black ant came out of the water and stopped to meet the gigantic face. They looked at each other in recognition. The tiny life, pleased and comforted, effortlessly moved along her hand and extended itself to the world.

CPSIA information can be obtained
at www.ICGtesting.com
Printed in the USA
LVHW010724201118
597698LV00001B/8/P